THE STRANGE RETURN OF
SHERLOCK HOLMES

THE STRANGE RETURN OF SHERLOCK HOLMES

Barry Grant

This first world edition published 2010
in Great Britain and in the USA by
SEVERN HOUSE PUBLISHERS LTD of
9–15 High Street, Sutton, Surrey, England, SM1 1DF.
Trade paperback edition published
in Great Britain and the USA 2010 by
SEVERN HOUSE PUBLISHERS LTD

British Library Cataloguing in Publication Data

Grant, Barry.
  The Strange Return of Sherlock Holmes.
  1. Retirees – England – Herefordshire – Fiction.
  2. Roommates – Fiction. 3. Holmes, Sherlock (Fictitious
  character) – Fiction. 4. Detective and mystery stories.
  I. Title
  823.9'2-dc22

ISBN-13: 978-0-7278-6887-9   (cased)
ISBN-13: 978-1-84751-236-9   (trade paper)

Severn House Publishers support The Forest Stewardship Council [FSC],
the leading international forest certification organisation. All our titles that
are printed on Greenpeace-approved FSC-certified paper carry the FSC logo

All Severn House titles are printed on acid-free paper.

Mixed Sources
Product group from well-managed
forests and other controlled sources
www.fsc.org Cert no. SA-COC-1565
© 1996 Forest Stewardship Council
FSC

Typeset by Palimpsest Book Production Ltd.,
Grangemouth, Stirlingshire, Scotland.
Printed and bound in Great Britain by
MPG Books Ltd., Bodmin, Cornwall.

*I gratefully inscribe this volume
to my grandfather, August,
who read Shakespeare,
Pope and pulp crime fiction
with equal gusto, and whose library
inspired me as a child to revel in life's mystery.*

ONE
Mr Cedric Coombes

In the year 2007 my wife left me for an American computer expert and flew away with him to Connecticut. At first I was depressed, for we had been married nearly thirty years. But I quickly got a grip on myself and determined to look as cheerful as I could. I decided this was my chance to indulge in adventures I had long contemplated but never undertaken. Straightaway I asked my editor to assign me to cover the war in Afghanistan, and although he was reluctant because of my age, he finally was persuaded. Within a month I had sold my London house, put my dog in the care of a neighbour, and was on an airplane to India. India had intrigued me ever since childhood, and I had decided to enjoy a month of travel in that fabled land before taking up my duties as a war correspondent. I visited Lucknow, Kanpur and other places where great battles had been fought by British troops in those faraway days when Britain ruled the waves and much of the world. As I stood by the Ganges at Varanasi, and by the desert at Jaipur, I had the strange feeling I'd been here before. Perhaps it was Kipling. I had read Kipling as a child, and he had made me feel almost as if I'd grown up in India.

I regretted that I was unable to enter Afghanistan through the Khyber Pass, the route by which our troops had entered in 1878, fighting their way – yard by bloody yard – at the outset of the second Afghan war. The stories of that campaign had always excited me and I was anxious to walk the ground. Everyone told me, however, that travelling through the Khyber was impossible. I took the usual air route to Afghanistan, landed in Kandahar and reported to 6th Division Headquarters in early September, full of high

hopes and good cheer. I had no inkling what bad luck and
bad dreams lay in store for me. I had vaguely anticipated
the horrors of war, but my knowledge had all come from
talk and from pale words on a page. To see maimed men
hobbling and dead people rotting, to see hungry cats
crawling out of corpses, to see citizens weeping with fear
and troops collapsing of wounds, is to know a different
truth than the one told in books. I was attached to the Royal
Horse Artillery and for three days I interviewed soldiers
and filed dispatches to my newspaper, and all went well.
Then I fell ill from dysentery and was forced to return to
Kandahar where I lay in a twilit world for several weeks
until at last my miseries ceased. Next I was assigned to the
Household Cavalry. Our squadron of light tanks floated and
jounced merrily across the desert landscape, and somehow
– amidst all the mayhem, dust and discomfort – I occasionally found some pleasant moments. But then as we passed
through a valley I stood up too high and was hit in the
shoulder by a sniper's bullet that shattered bone, grazed the
subclavian artery, and knocked me down so forcefully that
I thought, before I blacked out, that I was dead. The jolting
ride to the field hospital soon reminded me, sharply, that I
was still alive . . . unfortunately, as I then thought.

I lay for a long time in various hospitals. I knew that in
the vast scheme of things my injury was only minor. In the
bed next to mine lay a young soldier who never spoke a
word, just stared. He had lost both legs. Across the hallway
was a man who had suffered burns. He screamed unmer-
cifully whenever he wasn't moaning. He had, I think, lost
his mind. This entire war – concocted as it was by men
who all their lives had never done anything but hide in the
safety of their national borders – was such a disaster that
I should have guessed in advance that my part in it would
be a pointless debacle. My performance as a war correspondent had been dismal. I had sent very few dispatches
to my newspaper, and not one of them had seemed worthy
of the reality which surrounded me.

When I returned to England I took a few months to recuperate and get my bearings, then made my decision: I retired

from the newspaper and resolved to spend my days amidst green hills and good books, and to indulge in life's less turbulent pleasures. My life had changed utterly. I no longer had a wife, a house or even a dog, for now my little hound preferred my neighbour. I had neither obligations nor regrets. In brief, I was free to do whatever I could afford. I considered emigrating to America and 'holing up' in a cabin in the Wind River Range. I also imagined finding a small cottage in one of the old British Hill Stations of India – Simla, perhaps – and passing my days in a replica of the nineteen-thirties. Hills or mountains seemed to be the common denominator. One morning I awoke with a start, remembering a curious little place in Wales set in the hills just across the border from Herefordshire. It was a castle town with winding streets, bell tower, good pubs, and many antiquarian book shops. I had passed through there ten years earlier, and it had seemed to me a Kingdom of Books. The thought appealed. Hills for the heart, books for the brain. I packed my car, settled my lease, and left London.

On a blowy October evening, just as the sun was setting behind the hills, I arrived in Hay-On-Wye, slid into a shadowy parking spot behind the Old Black Lion Inn, and booked a room at that venerable hostelry. No reservation needed. I began to think that to plan life's journeys was to ruin them. *Consider the lilies of the field, how they grow . . .*

Days were sometimes dull with fog and rain, sometimes sharp with shadow and sun. I spent most mornings rambling steep hill paths, afternoons browsing bookshops, evenings eating fine food, and late nights travelling through Shakespeare, Tacitus and Newton in vain hope of becoming a half-educated man. One day I was standing in the Black Lion Bar when someone tapped me on the shoulder. Turning, I recognized Percy Ffoulkes, who had been a schoolmate of mine at Eton and later at Oxford. He was several years my junior and we had never been particular cronies, but seeing him appear so unexpectedly here in the wilds of Wales caused me to greet him with great enthusiasm, and he likewise seemed delighted at our surprise encounter. In a burst of good feeling I invited him to lunch. As we strolled up Bear Street he said, 'What have you been up to, Wilson! You look like ten pounds lighter than you did at college.'

'Illness does wonders for the waistline,' I said, and I briefly described the recent cataclysmic circumstances that had landed me in Wales.

'Poor fellow,' he said. 'But if a man your age is mad enough to allow himself to be shipped off to the Afghan War – well, you're lucky you were no more than wounded. What you up to now?'

'I've decided to stay the winter in this little town, if I can,' I replied. 'But I'll go broke if I remain at the Old Black Lion. I'm looking for a decent little cottage to rent at reasonable rates.'

'How odd,' remarked Ffoulkes. 'You are the second man today I've heard say that same thing.'

'And who was the first?'

'A fellow I literally bumped into at the Castle Bookshop. Later I encountered him again at the Poetry Book Store, and I asked him if he had had any luck finding lodgings. He said he had located a rental property right in town, but he needed someone to go halves with him, or else he could not afford it.'

'I wish I knew him,' I said. 'I wouldn't mind a roommate.'

Percy Ffoulkes looked at me with a sceptical smile as he set down his wine glass. 'I'm not sure you'd want this chap as a constant companion.'

'Something wrong with him?'

'I can't say that. But he certainly has a few quirks.'

'Such as?'

'Evidently he buys books by the hundreds at several book-stores in town, but only agrees to buy them "on approval." He loads them into a wheelbarrow and wheels them to his lodgings. About a week later he returns with most of the load, having kept only a few. The bookseller who told me this is one of several in town who have agreed to give him a refund on whatever he doesn't want to keep. The book-sellers don't like it, but he buys enough books to make it worth their while.'

'A wheelbarrow!'

'A regular garden wheelbarrow. I saw it with my own eyes.'

'Anything else odd about him?'

'I don't know. Would you call it odd, Wilson, if a man habitually analyzed books and pretended to be able to tell tales of their previous owners? That's one of his habits. I saw him do it. He was buying seven books out of the barrow load, and he laid one on the table and said to the book-seller, "This volume has a curious history: it was owned by a parson from Suffolk who purchased it in 1890 and gave it to his secret mistress, next owned by an elderly piano teacher from Bath who used sugar in her tea, then owned by a corrupt bank official who smoked Havana cigars and was imprisoned in 1950. And it is now about to be owned by a dead man."'

'That certainly is odd,' I admitted.

'He seemed amused at his joke about the dead man, if joke it was.'

'Some people are like that,' I said. 'They amuse themselves with harmless lies. Remember little Tony Stamford, at Eton?'

'Oh, heavens! I haven't thought of him in years,' cried Ffoulkes. 'The lies he used to tell!'

'Whatever happened to Tony, I wonder?'

'Twenty years ago I heard something about him taking up a post in Singapore. I forget who I heard it from. Ye gods, how old we have become, Wilson!'

'Remember how earnest we were? We were so anxious to learn. For we felt that before Eton we were too young to think, and soon we would be too busy, and eventually we would be too old. The golden time, we thought, was *now*. And now that *now* is nearly half a century ago.'

'I used to admire you greatly, Wilson – captain of the rowing team, and all that. We younger boys looked up to you.'

'You know Ffoulkes, those Eton days seem so distant that I remember them almost as if they were a tale I read in a book, rather than a life I really lived.'

'Yes, yes,' he said, and he looked bemused, seeming struck by the idea. He took a sip of wine. 'That's exactly how it feels – like a story I've read. Seeing myself from the outside, like a character in a story, or a movie. How curious!'

'I have,' I said, 'often asked people to remember a long-ago scene, and then I ask them whether they see that scene from within themselves or if they actually look at themselves from the outside, as in a movie. Ninety per cent say the latter.'

'It is hard to believe it's been almost half a century since we were standing on Eton Bridge and pegging biscuits to the swans. You're right – I see myself from the outside, a little boy in a uniform, standing there and looking down at the winking water. Say, this food is rather good.'

'You'll be around for a while, Ffoulkes?'

'I'm afraid not. I came just last evening, and in the morning I must drive back to London.'

'You didn't happen to hear where that strange chap was staying at present, did you?'

'No, but the bookseller would surely be able to – but wait, I do know. I remember him saying he was staying at Oxford Cottage.'

I asked the waitress where Oxford Cottage was located. She gave me directions, saying it was only a few minutes' walk. I paid the bill and a moment later we were out on the street in a flood of autumn sunshine, and a ghost of leaves was scurrying along the kerb ahead of us.

'The funny thing is,' said Ffoulkes, 'as I was watching that fellow I continually had the feeling that I knew him, that I had seen him before. As if perhaps he were a movie star, or a celebrity of some sort. But I can't place him. And yet I'm sure I've seen him, or someone very like him.'

'How old is this chap? If he's young I doubt he'd be interested in rooming with an old guy like me.'

'About our age, I expect. But don't get your hopes up. He is a very queer duck. As he was leaving the shop he asked the bookseller where he might purchase Fussell's Milk in *solderless sterilized tins*. Can you imagine that? Solderless sterilized tins. He said he always likes to keep a supply of Fussell's Milk for emergencies.'

'I've never heard of Fussell's Milk,' I said.

'Nor has anyone,' said Ffoulkes, with a laugh.

'He must have some deep research study under way,' I said, 'if it requires wheelbarrows full of books. Yet what could he be studying that couldn't be studied more efficiently at a bona fide research library? We have enough of those in this country.'

'I wondered the same thing, and after our strange friend had left the shop I asked the bookseller that very question. So far as he could tell, the man is interested in all history from 1914 to the present day, with particular emphasis on pop culture and science.'

We had now reached the top of the street, and we turned right into a busier road. After a little distance we reached Oxford Cottage and rang the bell. An empty wheelbarrow was parked out front. At the second ring, the door opened and a tall man about my own age – early sixties – stood before us, looking quizzical and just a little querulous. Like my friend Ffoulkes, I instantly had the impression that I had seen him somewhere before, though I couldn't imagine where. He was tall, slender – almost emaciated – with bright active eyes that glanced up, down, this way, that way, as if to take in every separate detail of me, and also every detail of Ffoulkes and the street behind us. His eyes I found a little unnerving, though his thin lips were smiling. His manner was genial enough, though tinged with impatience, as if he had many things pressing on his mind. He had a hawk nose and sharp chin, and made a pleasant impression despite his intensity of look and manner.

'Good day, gentleman,' said he. 'Who might you be looking for? I believe all the other guests are out at the moment.'

'I believe it is you we are looking for,' said I. 'My name is James Wilson. My friend here, Mr Percy Ffoulkes, recently overheard you wishing for someone to share the cost of a cottage.'

'Yes, yes, I remember you, Ffoulkes. You bumped into me at the bookshop.'

'That's it,' said Ffoulkes.

'I'm Cedric Coombes. By all means come inside, gentlemen, and let us get better acquainted.' He opened wide the
door and led us into a rather gloomy sitting room. As he did
so I noticed he had a slight limp in his left leg.

'I couldn't help overhear your comment about wishing
for a roommate,' said Ffoulkes. 'So when my friend here
mentioned that he was seeking inexpensive lodgings, I
thought we should look you up.'

'I'm not much of a host, gentlemen. I have nothing to
offer you from the kitchen, but please do make yourselves
comfortable.'

'Thank you,' I said, taking a seat on the sofa.

'I have found a very nice holiday cottage just around the
corner in Chancery Lane. It is too pricey for me to rent on
my own, and that is why I am looking for someone to share.
My intention is to settle there for the next two or three
months, where I can do my experiments more comfortably
than I can here.'

'Experiments?' said I.

'Excuse me,' cried Ffoulkes, 'do you smell something
burning!'

'Oh, no!' cried Coombes. 'I forgot.'

He leapt to his feet and, in several jerky steps, rushed
into the kitchen while we followed close behind. He
hurried to the stove where several sheets of paper in a
flat pan had burst into flames. He removed the pan and
set it in the sink, and black ash floated upward towards
the ceiling.

Ffoulkes was leaning in the doorway with his hands in
his pockets and a grin on his face. 'So that's what you do
with your wheelbarrows full of books,' he said. 'You slice
them up and burn them on the stove?' Ffoulkes nodded
towards the kitchen table where a book and a knife lay. The
book had been torn apart.

'Oh, a little hobby of mine,' said Coombes. 'It is possible
to learn a great deal more from books than what is printed in
them. I'm just carrying that notion to its logical conclusion.
I'm trying to develop a process to determine scientifically who
has owned, or handled, any book in the world.'

'And what,' said Ffoulkes, 'could be the point in doing that – even if it could be done?'

'Why, good Heavens!' cried Coombes. 'Had a test to prove who has handled a particular book or document been invented long ago, thousands of criminals now walking free would instead be paying the penalty for their crimes – criminals of every sort, from murderers to white-collar swindlers.'

'Do you have a theory how such a test might be constructed?' I asked.

'Several,' said he. 'They depend on identifying actual or reconstitutable samples of DNA found in the oils that the fingers leave on the pages of the book, or in flecks of skin that inevitably rub off when one is turning pages.'

'Sounds far-fetched,' said Ffoulkes, lazily. 'But good luck.'

'Oh, no, Mr Ffoulkes! A hundred years ago it would have been far-fetched. Today it is almost inevitable.'

'Really?' Ffoulkes smiled.

Coombes wiped his blackened hands on a towel and darted away into the sitting room with amazing speed, and then he vanished into a bedroom off the front hall. He returned with a book in his hands. 'I imagine you have read this book? *The Double Helix* by James D. Watson. I knew a man named Watson once. No relation, I'm sure. There has been a biological revolution, gentlemen, that astonishes me. They are cloning animals. They have created rat hearts using cells of baby rats. They have created mature human embryos from adult skin cells. I am sure you know all this.'

'Yes, yes, it is all very amazing,' said Ffoulkes. 'But on a more practical note, what sort of place is this holiday cottage you have found?'

'Quite right, quite right,' apologized Coombes. 'I get too excited when my favourite topics are in the air. The cottage has two bedrooms, a sitting room, kitchen, bathroom, patio, and a nice view of the hills. That's about all I can say. I think you will like it, Mr Wilson. The main thing is, will you like me? Perhaps I should enumerate my worst traits.'

'I don't think that is necessary,' I said, laughing.

But Coombes was determined to tell me his faults. 'I'm moody,' he said. 'I'm alternately in a state of furious energy and then in a state of reverie and passivity, a dreamlike state. What we used to call "a brown study".'

'What do you do in your furious state?' I asked.

'Walk the floor, dart away to solve problems, talk too much. I have learnt my behaviour can be disconcerting to those who are used to regularity and steady habits.'

'I do need peace. My nerves are easily jangled. Are you ever loud?'

'I am loud only when I play the violin,' said he. 'And I haven't played a violin since . . . well, I haven't played one for a long time. But I intend to obtain one as soon as possible.'

'Do you play well?'

'Exquisitely, if I do say so myself,' said Coombes. 'Anyway, I used to play exquisitely. But I can assure you, Watson . . .'

'Wilson.'

'Sorry, yes. Wilson. I can assure you that if I find I no longer play the violin exquisitely, I will instantly give it up. A violin played less than perfectly is too painful to bear. I could not put myself through the agony – much less anyone else.'

'That's all right, then. Any other faults?'

'Not that I can think of.'

I had to laugh at his logical approach to this whole problem, as if setting up a balance sheet of pluses and minuses would really help anyone decide anything. But I had decided to go along with his fantasy.

'So it is my turn to confess,' I said. 'Then, I must tell you, first of all, that I am opinionated. I try to restrain myself from voicing my opinions when they are not wanted, but I do not always succeed.'

'I don't mind wrong opinions. I find them amusing,' said Coombes.

'Also, I am by nature impatient.'

'So am I,' said Coombes.

'Third, I stay up very late and rise very early, and though

I will promise to be as quiet as a mouse, I cannot change the sleep habits of a lifetime.'

'Sometimes I don't go to bed at all,' said Coombes.

'Well, there we are,' said Ffoulkes, smiling and rubbing his hands together like a broker who has just seen his clients conclude a deal.

'If you are agreeable,' said Coombes, 'we can meet at the property tomorrow at nine, so you can decide whether it suits you. I'll call the agent.'

'Excellent,' I said.

Coombes gave me a sheet describing the cottage and how to find it. Then we shook hands and he said, 'Everyone talks so much about Afghanistan these days. How did you like it there?'

'I confess,' said I, 'that it was not . . . I say, but how did you know that I . . .?'

The doorbell rang again and Coombes hurried to answer it. An old woman wearing a backpack was on the front stoop. 'Is this Oxford Cottage?' she asked. 'I have a reservation.'

While Coombes showed the woman into the kitchen to await the arrival of the manager, Ffoulkes and I left and strolled back towards the centre of town.

'By the way,' I said, suddenly stopping and turning to Ffoulkes, 'how in the world did he know I had been to Afghanistan?'

'I don't think either of *us* told him.'

'No, I'm sure we didn't. But it was curious, wasn't it? And then all this folderol about cooking books to learn their owners – I don't know what to make of him.'

'Nor do I,' said Ffoulkes. 'But he seems harmless enough. And anyway, Wilson, you always liked puzzles when we were at school. Mr Cedric Coombes is a puzzle you can work out in your spare time, when you tire of buying first editions of Dickens and hiking the foggy hills.'

We walked to the car park by the tourist information centre and said our goodbyes, and we vowed to meet up in London someday soon – one of those vows old friends make in the heat of sudden meeting, but seldom carry out.

Percy Ffoulkes climbed into his Range Rover, waved, and through the window his face seemed suddenly young, as I had known it years ago in the flower of our youth. And then he was gone in a swirl of leaves.

I walked towards the Boz Books shop, anxious to examine a first edition of *Pickwick Papers* that I had found there – and anxious, also, for morning to arrive so I could learn more about my curious new acquaintance.

TWO
The Logic of Poetical Leaps

I met Coombes next day in Chancery Lane, as he had
arranged, in front of a pretty stone cottage in a row of
stone cottages that walled one side of the street. Cambrai
Cottage featured a sitting room with a wood-beamed ceiling
and a large stone fireplace. At the top of the stairs were
two bedrooms, one looking on to the street, the other on
to the patio behind the house. We were pleased by the prem-
ises and by the price which, when divided by two, was
quite reasonable. We concluded our bargain on the spot.
On that very morning I checked out of the Old Black Lion
and moved my belongings into Cambrai Cottage. The
following morning Coombes arrived with his wheelbarrow
of books and a very ancient leather suitcase with three faded
stickers on the side. Only one of the stickers could still be
read: *Hotel Beau-Rivage, Quai du Mont-Blanc, Geneve.*

Coombes was certainly an easy enough man to live with.
He rose early but never made a sound. He waited until I
was away hiking the hills before conducting his book
experiments in the kitchen. These experiments involved
heating pages of books, then putting them into a bath of
chemicals. But he made it a point to clean up the mess
before I arrived back for lunch. His books were numerous
but never in the way. He kept them carefully stacked in
and around the bookcase at one side of the sitting room,
and he carried them off to his bedroom in piles of five or
six. Often when I arrived back in the evening I found him
sitting in front of a roaring fire and reading three books
simultaneously, going from one to the other as he apparently compared them. He seemed like a man in mad pursuit
of something or other, but of *what* remained a mystery to
me. In the titles he collected I could see no pattern. He

had biographies of the Beatles, Tony Blair, Bill Gates, Bertrand Russell and many others. He had histories of World War I, World War II, the Korean War, the Falklands War, the current wars in Iraq and Afghanistan, plus histories of England, France, the United States, China, and various other countries – but none of these histories covered any period earlier than the twentieth century. Most numerous were books on modern science and technology, including quantum theory, global warming, alternative energy sources, acupuncture, mental illness and computers. Many books on computers. Also books on the biological sciences, especially genetic engineering of all sorts, including recombinant DNA cloning and reproductive cloning. In one corner was a pile of books on hypnotism, hallucinatory drugs, spiritualism and meditation. In another corner I noticed books on Marilyn Monroe, the history of sport in the twentieth century, the history of aviation, and a textbook on organic chemistry.

What was he aiming at? Surely he had to have some specific goal, I thought. No man buys and borrows books by the barrowful without a definite purpose. But what that purpose might be I could not make out. There was a certain reserve in our relationship that prevented me from asking him outright. We roomed together, often ate together, but we carefully respected each other's privacy – perhaps as a way of keeping our own secrets. We were, after all, two men of more than sixty who were perhaps reluctant to press each other about our *goals in life* at a period when, as everyone knows, goals often tend to fizzle and life to become a mere habit. Maybe he was just pottering, piddling and fiddling away his time with unusual intensity.

Yet somehow I doubted it.

As he had warned me, he periodically fell from a frenzied state of mind into a mood of lassitude, and for several days on end he would lie on the couch and stare into space, scarcely seeming to be aware of me when I entered the room. On one such day I had walked in, apparently unnoticed, and was sitting by the fire engrossed in the sports pages of the *Guardian* when his voice startled me:

'What do you think of the opinion piece on page thirty, the one titled "The Missing Illogical Leap"?'

'I haven't read it,' said I, 'but I will.'

I turned to the article and read it briskly.

'What is your opinion of it?' asked Coombes, anxiously.

'So far as I can tell,' I said, 'it is an argument that relies more on sophistry than good sense, and tries to prove a point that is almost true but not quite.'

'Really?'

'The writer appears to believe that computers can never compete with the human mind, and why? Because, he argues, they cannot make the illogical leaps of imagination necessary in order to solve life's big mysteries. That sounds like philosophical twaddle. Surely life's mysteries never required illogical leaps in order to be solved.'

'Perhaps the article wasn't written as clearly as it might be,' said Coombes, frowning.

'The writer sounds like someone of the old school who refuses to accept reality, which is that computers have over-taken human intelligence, and will continue to sprint ahead of our plodding brains. We all once believed that no computer could beat a Grand Master at chess – but computers now do this every day. We all used to think that abstruse problems could only be solved by a philosopher, but recently many mathematical problems that have defeated mathematical philosophers for centuries have been solved by computers.'

'Small problems may have been solved,' objected Coombes. 'But for the greatest mysteries of life, computers are useless.'

'I am willing to be convinced,' I said, smiling. I had never seen Coombes so excited. He was almost frothing.

'Computers are mere compilers and crunchers of facts. Yet facts alone, Watson . . .'

'Wilson . . .'

'. . . can never, however speedily compiled or crunched, solve anything of consequence.'

'I wonder what you mean, Coombes, by *of consequence*. Perhaps we are not really in disagreement.'

'I mean any of the great mysteries of life. The mystery of gravity, for instance. Or the mystery of why a man murders his wife. Many years ago I too believed such problems could be solved merely by observing closely and analyzing logically. I believed that a problem was like a great river one must cross. You stood on the shore and by stepping from one logical stepping stone to the next, you eventually reached the far side.'

'But that *is* how it is done, isn't it?' I said.

'Not at all. In every mystery I ever solved – and I have solved a number of minor mysteries – I proceeded in a completely different manner. I lived a whole lifetime before realizing this. That is why I wrote the article.'

'*You* wrote it!' I cried, opening the paper again. 'I guess I am not very observant. I was in such a hurry to read the piece that . . .'

'Oh, most people are too much in a hurry to observe properly. It's a human trait,' laughed Coombes. 'Anyway, long ago I imagined that I solved mysteries first by observing, then by analyzing facts I had accumulated by observing. But that is not how it is at all. I realize now that I always made an imaginative leap that landed me somewhere strange, and then I tried to prove by logic that my leap had landed me in the right spot. If not, I made another leap, till eventually I landed where logic could prove I was spot on.'

'I'm afraid I must differ with you, Coombes,' I said. 'I think it has long been established that sharp observation and careful analysis provide more solutions than leaps of fancy. I leave fancy to the poets. It is science which has built our world. Men like Newton, and Henry Ford, and Bill Gates.'

'But Newton was a poet.'

'Come now, Coombes!'

'But just think of how he worked! He saw surprising and hidden likenesses, just as poets do. For instance, he saw a round red apple and a round white moon, and he saw the apple falling from the sky while the moon did not fall but only circled. Those were his facts. Had he only analyzed those facts he would have learnt nothing. But he made an imaginative leap and guessed what he later proved – that the apple fell towards the earth for the same reason that the moon fell around the earth. Gravity was the link that neither he nor anyone could have proved until first he had guessed it. His guess was his imaginative leap.'

'If you are referring only to cosmic questions, perhaps you are right. But Newton is an unusual case,' I said.

'Not at all,' said Coombes. 'I have concluded that the plague of this new age is a mindless trust in artificial intelligence. Men ought to trust instead to their own brains and instincts. I don't speak only of cosmic questions, the meaning of life or the origin of the universe. I speak of small things, daily life – the solving of a crime or the solving of a personal problem with a . . . a *lover*, I suppose you now would call it. A man with powers of observation, analysis and imagination should – to take a trivial example – be able to deduce a great deal about a person from some small object that the person owned – say his watch or his car keys. But feeding data about that object into a computer would lead to nothing at all.'

'That is surely an interesting theory,' I admitted. 'But I'll wager that you could not conclude anything significant about a person merely by examining an object the individual owns.'

'You would lose your wager,' said Coombes.

'Then let me put you to the test,' I said.

'Certainly,' said Coombes. 'I have had a boring day and need some stimulation.'

'Here is a pocket knife owned by my brother Charles,' I said, pulling it out of a drawer. 'He was working in Europe – he is an archaeologist – and he stopped by to visit me on his way back to Chicago where he teaches at a university. He has travelled with this old knife since college days and he did not want to lose it by checking it through with his luggage, which airline regulations would force him to do. The airline has lost two of his bags in the last two years. So he asked me to send the knife to him when he arrived home. I was going to post it tomorrow.'

'Ah,' said Coombes. 'If you will be good enough to give it to me, I shall try to demonstrate that my theory is practical.'

I handed him my brother's old Swiss Army knife and he eagerly carried it away to the front window where evening sunlight, falling through the panes, made a bright patch on the table. He laid the knife in the patch of sunlight, sat down at the table, and from somewhere he produced a large magnifying glass that looked like the sort of antique magnifier that Charles Darwin might have used while exploring the Galapagos, or that Linnaeus might have peered through while squatting over *Galeopsis ladanum*. The rim was tarnished brass and the handle was of wood so worn by handling that it shone. As I watched him peering into that magnifying glass – his hawk nose, his angular figure – I again had the feeling that I had seen this man somewhere before. But where I could not say.

Coombes studied the knife with painful care, turning its smooth red form over and over in his hands as if fondling it. At last he drew out the tiny tweezers from their tiny slot and examined them with his glass. Then he laid them aside on a Kleenex and withdrew the white toothpick from its compartment and examined it with equal attention. He opened each of the blades and accessories and examined each with excruciating care – the big blade, the small blade, the screwdriver-and-bottle-opener blade, then the can-opener-and-tiny-screwdriver blade, and finally the saw blade. With a toothpick he teased out wads of fuzzy material caught in the cavity where those blades had resided, and examined it under the glass. Next he turned the knife over and examined the final two blades – the awl and the corkscrew.

What a lot of show and fuss, I was thinking.

Then he began shaking his head, and it was obvious to me that his project was a failure. I couldn't pretend to myself that I was sorry. He had taken on the air of a pedant as he had lectured me on the nature of knowledge, as though I were a child. I don't like to see anyone humiliated, but I was glad he had been deflated a bit.

Coombes finally closed the knife and looked at me with a sigh. 'I fear I've promised more than I can perform, Wilson.'

'Ah, well,' said I.

'The knife did not reveal as much as I had hoped.'

'Think nothing of it, Coombes,' said I, magnanimously. 'We all miscalculate occasionally.'

'Still, my research has not been entirely barren,' he said.

'By all means, then,' I said, 'let me hear what the knife has revealed – if anything.'

Coombes solemnly handed the knife back to me and sat down in the easy chair by the fire. He placed both his bony elbows on the cushioned arms of the chair, then threw his head back, pressed his finger tips together, and stared at the ceiling with his mouth open slightly and the tip of his tongue between his teeth. In this dramatic pose he remained for an intolerable while. Again I grew impatient. Theatrics are fine, so long as one doesn't overdo them. Then I smiled and suddenly the whole scene struck me as amusing. Could it be that Coombes had been on the stage, perhaps as a magician or an old member of the RSC? Could that be where I had seen him before? How odd, I thought, that I had lived with the man for several weeks and still knew nothing whatever about his background!

'All that I can say with any confidence,' said Coombes, 'is that he is a man of about fifty with dark hair that has begun to grow grey, and a man who is very particular about his looks. He is impatient yet also careful. He is frugal, meticulous and sentimental. He likes wine and frequently buys a bottle to drink during his travels, but he seldom drinks beer. He sketches using a number 2B – or perhaps HB – drawing pencil.' Coombes looked at me wearily and drew a deep breath. 'That is really all I can say, other than that your brother recently has been bathing on Kamari beach on Santorini, that he passed through Switzerland on his way to England, that he has a Persian cat at his house in Chicago, and that he is a member of the Masons.'

I suddenly felt almost sick. I felt invaded. 'I am shocked, Coombes,' I said. 'I like a good joke as well as any man, and I will take this whole episode as a joke – but when you begin reading someone else's mail . . . well, that is really inexcusable. Even for a joke. I am a lighthearted person, Coombes. I am not easily offended. Many people have told me I am an easy man to get along with. But we will not get along very well if we cannot trust each other.'

'I did not read your mail,' he said, looking rather startled.

'But my good fellow, it is obvious you must have.'

'Absolutely not. How can you deduce such a thing?'

I began to feel confused about having accused him. 'Well, come to think, in his letter my brother didn't mention his Persian cat . . . and also he didn't . . . but how in the world did you . . . because every word of your description is correct. You spoke as if you might know him personally, and be acquainted with his character and habits and all his affairs. Please enlighten me, Coombes.'

'Nothing easier,' he replied, waving his thin hand through the air in the manner of a showman. 'You mentioned that your brother was a great deal younger than you, an archae-ologist from Chicago. In my reading during the past several months I have twice come across the name of the famous archaeologist C.D. Wilson, a professor in Chicago who specializes in studying the excavated Cretan town of Akrotiri on Santorini. Almost certainly your brother Charles is that same C.D. Wilson. So when I found black sand amongst the debris in his pocket knife, it was not much of a leap to imagine he visited the black sand beach of Kamari on Santorini.'

'That's true,' I said. 'He complained that he got sunburnt there, even though it was late in the season and the air seemed cool.'

'The knife is at least thirty years old,' Coombes continued, 'and you have told me you are sixty-four. A little math-ematical juggling shows that if your brother is, say, ten to fifteen years younger than you, he would now be forty-nine to fifty-four – and if we subtract the age of the knife from that estimated age, we deduce that he acquired the knife when he was in his late teens or early twenties, which fits with the notion he acquired it at college. That his hair is dark stands to reason since yours is dark. I know that it has begun to turn grey because I found a single grey nose hair stuck to the inside of the tweezer. A man who troubles himself to pluck nose hairs is obviously more fastidious about his looks than most of us are. The two knife blades were carefully sharpened to a razor edge, which suggests the owner is both meticulous and orderly – and the fact he kept the knife for more than thirty years suggests he is both careful and frugal. The handle has been cracked and repaired – a fact which might suggest he is also sentimental, since many a man in his position would simply have purchased a new knife. He obviously wished to keep his old friend in his pocket.

'As to the rest, I observed a bit of cork still on the corkscrew, indicating that at least on his last bottle of wine he forcefully pulled the screw straight out of the cork instead of screwing it out. This suggests he is sometimes impatient, despite his generally careful habits. The corkscrew was worn shiny but the bottle opener after thirty years had not the tiniest scratch on it, suggesting that while he liked wine he seldom drank beer – beer in a bottle, anyway, which is usually how it is sold in Europe. Fine bits of pencil lead clung to the small blade, and few people use pencils these days except for drawing, and fewer still have occasion to sharpen them with their pocket knife, but an artist might need to do this quite often if he is sketching in the field – as I do myself. When I rubbed them they smeared moderately easily, and long experience with pencil lead leads me to think he uses 2B to HB. Whether your brother Charles sketches as part of his archaeological activities or purely for pleasure, or both, I do not know.

'Two Persian cat hairs beneath much of the fuzz in the knife cavity suggested a cat at home, and of course the tiny Masonic medallion attached to the ring of the knife would only be carried by a member of the lodge. Finally, a piece of paper currency had become wedged in the saw blade, and your brother – his impatience again – just tore it free without opening the knife. This left a tiny fragment of paper stuck to the blade. I have made a study of European currency and recognized both the colour and paper texture as characteristic of a Swiss fifty-franc note. It is a shame that most of the other countries on the continent now use the Euro – it makes crime detection so much more difficult.'

'*Crime* detection?' I said.

'Or any sort of detection or deduction one might wish to make,' he added quickly.

THREE
The Mystery of the Black Priest

The next morning Coombes fell suddenly into one of his more and more frequent fits of depression. He slept late, no longer wheeled his barrow of books through the streets of Hay, no longer darted his eyes from object to object or lightly leapt from topic to topic in our conversations. In fact, he hardly spoke. He sat in front of the fireplace in his slippers and robe, and stared. Occasionally he rolled his eyes dreamily up in his head. This went on for several days, and then got worse. One morning, after having refused my offer of breakfast, he said, 'What I need, Watson . . .'

'Wilson . . .'

'. . . is a syringe of cocaine and a pipe of tobacco. My doctor allows me the cocaine but refuses to allow me the tobacco. I promised him I would abstain, but I fear I cannot stand this much longer. When I have no problems to solve, life has lost its meaning.' He looked frightful and distracted as he said this. He did not look healthy.

'Let me get you some tea,' I said.

'Thank you.'

'Or maybe some gin might do you good.'

'I have never used spirits,' he cried, 'but I may need to try them.' He flung himself on to the couch and put his hands behind his head and stared at the ceiling.

Beethoven's *Für Elise* suddenly began to play somewhere in the room, and I looked about, wondering. Coombes began digging in his sport coat pocket and, to my surprise, he pulled out a mobile phone. He struggled to open it. But *Für Elise* played on. I hurried to him and showed him how to manipulate the telephone. Awkwardly he held it to his ear. I discreetly withdrew to the kitchen, but I could not help but hear his end of the conversation. I gathered from some fragmentary words that he was speaking to someone in London. *I really don't know if I can wait until our appointment, that's a week away. . . . I've already lived longer than anybody else, which ought to guarantee me a few privileges, doctor . . . not so sure we should have undertaken this experiment . . . I don't need medicine, I need work . . . yes, by all means tell my contact at Scotland Yard . . . he is a kind man but I doubt he can help; chance provides more cures than kindness . . . do my best, of course . . . only the leg is a problem . . . and my mind, my mind . . . goodbye.*

I emerged from the kitchen with his cup of tea. I set it beside him but he didn't even see it. He stared into the fire. I threw another log into the flames and left him to his reveries while I fixed myself a small lunch and then went out for the afternoon.

When I returned home in the evening, Coombes sat just as he had been sitting when I left him. This worried me considerably. The tea was cold beside him.

'I say, Coombes, could you do for a little supper?'

No answer.

He seemed almost in a catatonic state or – if I wanted to characterize it a little more cheerfully – a state of deep meditation.

Eventually I climbed the stairs and went to bed, and for a while I lay awake listening for his footsteps. Then light rain began to fall on the roof, and lulled me to sleep, and I dreamt I was riding in a coach with Mr Pickwick who kept spilling his cake.

In the morning I was gratified to see that Coombes had moved during the night. The tea cup was in the kitchen sink. Cake crumbs on the counter indicated he had at last eaten something. I found him sitting on the little patio behind the house, all muffled up in his robe and jacket and slippers, watching the day bloom. Leaves occasionally skittered and flittered by his feet.

'Good morning, Coombes,' said I, looking as cheerfully unconcerned as possible. Then I walked up the street, bought a newspaper, and read it while sipping coffee in my favourite little restaurant. An hour or two later I returned to Cambrai and found Coombes still on the patio.

'Autumn days are the same in every century,' said he.

'Are you feeling better this morning?'

'I feel I am about to go mad,' he said, in a dull voice. 'I need something to happen, Wilson. I shall go mad – I am sure of it – if something doesn't happen soon.'

And just at that moment something happened. It was almost as if the gods had heard his request and instantly answered it, or as if we were in a stage play in which things always happen right on cue but too conveniently to be entirely believable. What happened was that Sergeant Bundle of the local constabulary lurched up into view behind the back gate and hailed Mr Coombes.

'Mr Coombes,' said he, stepping on to the patio. 'So there you are. Have you got a moment, sir?'

Coombes nodded, dully.

The sergeant wore a white shirt and tie, with bars on his shoulders, and he looked very spiffy and bluff and also a bit downcast. He smiled with his mouth but his eyes squinted in worry. 'Mr Coombes, I've just had a conversation with our mutual acquaintance at Scotland Yard – you know who I mean.'

'Yes, yes, I do.'

'Our mutual acquaintance informs me that you might be able to help us with a problem we have encountered here in Dyfed.'

'Yes?' said Coombes, looking up sharply.

'A murder, Mr Coombes.'

'Murder?'

'The gentleman at Scotland Yard has urged me to get into contact with you.' The sergeant raised a chubby hand. 'We don't exactly *need* your help, you understand, Mr Coombes. But this case has some very strange components. We feel we could use your suggestions.'

Coombes was suddenly transformed. He sprang to his feet and stood as rigidly as a grenadier, leaning forward slightly, his face intent. 'I will be very glad to assist you, if I am able.'

'And this gentleman?' said Sergeant Bundle, motioning to me affably.

'Quite safe, quite safe,' said Coombes. 'This is Mr James Wilson.'

After having established that it was safe to speak in front of me, we three sat around the metal table on the patio and Sergeant Bundle described his problem, leaning forward and holding his thick hands over the table top as if he were holding the problem itself – which appeared to be about the size of a large brick. He turned the problem over and over as he spoke, as if to reveal all of its aspects.

'Murder, Mr Coombes, is a common crime.'

'Indeed.'

'But this murder, sir, is baffling. There are no clues.'

'Pray give me the details.'

'I will try to be brief,' said Bundle. 'I know your time is valuable.'

'Actually, it is not terribly valuable,' said Coombes. 'I am interested in all details, however minute.'

'A young American named Calvin Hawes arrived in town last week, having come all the way from Georgia,' said Bundle. 'He booked a room for a week at the Swan Hotel on Belmont Road. Yesterday evening he asked the man at the front desk, Mr Twembley, for directions to The Old Vicarage cottage, which lies in a secluded lane just outside of town. Twembley thought it an odd request because he knew that Mr Jenkins, who owns The Old Vicarage, has been away in Scotland for the past month. But Twembley drew him a little map, just the same. Calvin Hawes also asked Mr Twembley if he knew of a family in town named *Languish*. Twembley said he did not. Hawes then wrote out the name *Languish* but Twembley assured him that although he had lived in town a quarter century he knew no such family. The young man asked if Mr Twembley knew a girl in town whose Christian name was . . . Linda? Sylvia? I forget. No matter.

'Calvin Hawes left the hotel about five o'clock, and Twembley noticed he was carrying a bouquet of flowers wrapped in gold paper, which Twembley thought charming but odd.

'I must now explain something, sir. It is this: a hiking path leads from the town into Brecon Beacons National Park, right up to Hay Bluff. This path climbs over the hill just behind The Old Vicarage, and from it you can see the upper storey of the cottage, though mainly what you see is the roof and the chimneys. Last evening, just at dusk, two of our townspeople were descending the mountain path with their dogs when they noticed a light on in The Old Vicarage. They thought that their friend David Jenkins must have come back from Scotland earlier than planned, and they called his house phone to greet him – intending, you know, to say that they were standing on the hill behind his house and looking at him through his windows. But he did not answer. They assumed he must be taking a bath or some such thing, and they left a message on his answering machine saying they would be coming round in a few minutes to welcome him back.

'These two descended the path to Oxford Road and drove in their Vauxhall round to Jenkins's place. But they could not rouse him. They went on home. But early this morning they telephoned Jenkins again. When he still did not answer they got concerned. They telephoned me at the station and asked if I would look in on The Old Vicarage. Officer Jones and I arrived there some hours ago. We found the place deserted. Several lights seemed to gleam within, but no one answered our knock. No vehicles were in the garage. Then we noticed that the front door had been jimmied and the lock broken. We pushed it open and went inside.

'At first we saw nothing at all. Nothing appeared disturbed. The doilies were all in place on the table tops, the clocks were ticking. We assumed a burglar had broken in but we could not see what had been stolen. All seemed in perfect order. Then, by sheer chance, we glanced into the bathroom and saw what I had never expected to see.

'I must now explain something, sir, and it is this: the tub in that bathroom is a very large tub, with lion feet. Over the top of that ancient tub had been laid a pane-glass door. It had been removed (as we later discovered) from where it had hung between the sitting room and the sun porch.

We looked down through the glass door and saw the corpse of Calvin Hawes in a rosy tubful of blood and water. One of the large panes of glass had been smashed and the man's throat had apparently been gashed by the smashed shards that still hung like knives in the frame. Apparently he had sat up in the tub to escape drowning, had smashed his head against the pane, broken it, and when he fell back again the shards just slit his throat. His hands were tied behind his back. When we lifted him out of the water we found he was clutching a bouquet of flowers in his bound hands – almost as if he meant to whisk them out from behind his back and surprise someone.'

'How odd,' said Coombes.

'There was one other odd thing,' said Bundle. 'On the mirror we found the word *Heigh-ho* written in soap.'

'Just that?' queried Coombes.

'Nothing more, sir. And that is about all there is to tell at this moment. We have collected the dead man's belongings from his hotel room. We are presently trying to retrieve messages from the hard drive of his laptop computer. The victim may have had some email communication with whoever killed him. At any rate, the desk clerk, Twembley, saw the victim working with his computer in the lounge of the hotel shortly before he left for The Old Vicarage.'

During Bundle's recitation of the facts Coombes had been sitting bolt upright in his chair with his hand on his chin and his index finger across his lips. Now he removed his finger. 'And you saw no other sign of the killer at all? Nothing but the words written on the mirror?'

'That is the puzzling part. We found nothing out of place except in that bathroom. Every other room appeared completely undisturbed. Not a single item was touched, not a single item damaged or out of place – except for the front door which, as I have said, had been jimmied and the lock broken. Mr Jenkins informed us – we telephoned him in Scotland – that it was he who had removed the sun porch door and leant it in the back hallway, intending to dispose of it when he returned from holiday. He no longer wants a door separating the sun porch.'

'When will Mr Jenkins return?' asked Coombes.

'That is anybody's guess,' said Bundle. 'He lives in the cottage only about one week each month. He is a theatrical producer in London. He comes and he goes.'

'Does he have neighbours?'

'Only Mrs Ogmore. She is ninety-five. I'm afraid she, at her age, is just a wee bit unreliable. She said she saw nothing last evening except Father Pritchard riding by on his bicycle.'

'When was that?'

'A little after dusk had settled on the hills. Unfortunately, Father Pritchard has been dead for eighty years. I doubt anyone in town ever knew him except her.'

'Ahh,' said Coombes. 'And has Mrs Ogmore ever seen the good Father on other occasions in recent years?'

'That I cannot tell you, Mr Coombes. I would not doubt that she has.'

'That could be an important detail,' said Coombes.

Bundle spread his thick fingers, suddenly letting drop the problem he had been turning over and over in his hands. He leant back in his chair, and grinned. 'Long ago, sir, our mutual acquaintance at Scotland Yard – you know who I mean – warned me that you were a man for detail. But I confess, sir, I am surprised, nonetheless, at the quantity of detail you require.'

'I wonder,' said Coombes, 'would you be good enough to allow me to have a look at the crime scene?'

'Certainly, sir,' said Bundle. 'It would be a pleasure.'

Coombes hurried to his room. A few minutes later he reappeared wearing a brown Harris tweed sport jacket with leather elbows, brown wool trousers, smooth leather shoes, a brown shirt open at the collar, and a plaid wool hat that made him look a little like Bing Crosby. Soon we were in Bundle's police car gliding along a deserted lane beyond the edge of town. Leaves whirled down and the bright sun was masked and unmasked by scudding clouds, and the whole landscape seemed to shrink and grow with the dimming and brightening of the light. Bundle pointed, 'There be Mrs Ogmore now, rake in hand.'

'Ah, may we have a word with her?' cried Coombes.

Bundle hit the brake and swung into the driveway.

Mrs Ogmore was raking briskly. She wore a large straw hat. She was thin, and her thin white dress blew, and she wore a green jacket that was too big for her. Coombes got out of the car and walked to her and the two of them stood amidst swirling leaves, facing each other a few feet apart. Bundle and I hurried up to them.

'My name is Cedric Coombes,' said Coombes. 'I'm working with Sergeant Bundle.'

'How do you do,' she said, and looked up at him with pressed lips as she nodded firmly.

'May I ask you a question?'

'Of course. You look like a sensible young man.' She smiled coquettishly.

'Have you often seen Father Pritchard riding his bicycle?'

'Not in recent years. He's been gone a long time.'

Here Sergeant Bundle raised a finger and interrupted. 'Now, think clearly, Constance,' he said. 'Think what you are saying. This morning you told me . . .'

'I am thinking perfectly clearly,' said Constance Ogmore. 'Father Pritchard has been dead for eighty years. The last time I saw him was in 1927 when I was fourteen years old. You are talking foolishness.'

'Ah,' said Coombes. 'But yesterday evening, just after dusk, did you see anyone riding a bicycle?'

'I don't remember seeing anyone,' she replied, in her high little voice. 'I do remember Father Pritchard used to ride a bicycle. He used to ride all round the countryside in his priestly robe.' Suddenly she chuckled. 'When the wind was up he looked like a bat! I shouldn't say such things, of course.'

'Thank you, Mrs Ogmore,' said Coombes.

Coombes left her – almost rudely, I thought, under the circumstances – and hurried to the car, limping wildly on his game leg.

Bundle put the car into gear. 'Lord, lord, poor woman,' he gasped as he backed out.

Fifty yards further down the lane we came to the drive leading to The Old Vicarage. Already the body had been removed from the house. Coombes walked carefully through every room, upstairs and downstairs, and with his ancient magnifying glass he examined table tops, floors, curtains. What he was looking for I could not imagine. On several occasions I noticed Sergeant Bundle standing with his hands on his fat hips, and with a self-satisfied smile on his face, gazing with amusement at the bent and urgent figure of Coombes. I had the feeling – once again – that Coombes reminded me of someone. I decided it must an actor in an old film. But I could not recall the film or the actor. Maddening.

The last room he examined was the bathroom. I had seen blood and death aplenty in Afghanistan, but the sight of a tub full of blood – a literal blood bath – unsettled me and I did not look at it closely. Coombes, however, was on his knees by the tub, carefully examining all the fixtures, every aspect of the room. To my surprise he suddenly produced a small digital camera from his pocket and began taking photographs, seeming to pay particular attention to the pane-smashed door which had been removed from the top of the tub and leant against a wall.

The cottage was furnished with an eclectic mix of ancient and modern objects, nineteenth century antiques and paintings cheek by jowl with modern appliances and modern art. Much of the art had a theatrical theme, reflecting the interests of a theatrical manager – photographs of Lawrence Olivier, John Barrymore, Vanessa Redgrave and other famous stage actors, a painting of Sarah Bernhardt, an engraving of David Garrick as Richard III by William Hogarth, and so on. Coombes lurched about with insect energy and only once did his attention seem to waver from the task at hand. He stopped suddenly and gazed at a box camera on one of the bookshelves in the study, and he said, 'Why, I had a camera like that. Do they still sell them?' Then he seemed to bethink himself, and he murmured, 'Surely not, no.'

'I'm sure you can find one in London, sir,' said Bundle, rocking back on his heels. 'Many an antique dealer specializes in cameras.'

'Yes, yes,' muttered Coombes, and he tilted his glass to examine a book more closely, without touching it.

'I'm sure I can't imagine what you are searching for,' said Bundle, his thick fingers fidgeting. I had noticed for some while that he had been growing impatient with the excruciating slowness of Coombes's examination.

'I may already have found it,' said Coombes. 'If you gentlemen would be good enough to come with me to the entry hall, I'll show you.'

On the entry table were a bust of Shakespeare and a bust of Voltaire, and between the two were artfully piled a number of old and new books. 'There is one book on this table that was put here recently,' said Coombes. 'You can see a fine layer of dust on the table itself, if you look against the light. That same dust is on each of the books, except one. This one.' He pointed to a closed book lying face down on the table.

'Well, sir?'

'Someone has put it here within the last day or so. It has a dark dust jacket, and dust would plainly show on it, if there were any. Also, if you look closely you will see that someone has not only set the book on to the table, but twisted it slightly, thus creating the shape of a small fan in the dust, where the book was turned.'

'Yes,' said Bundle, squinting and nodding. 'That is the case.'

'This book may well tell us a tale or two that the author never envisioned,' said Coombes. 'I should like to examine it more closely.'

Bundle stepped backwards a pace and held his arms wide, palms up. 'Help yourself, Mr Coombes.'

'Thank you.'

Bundle raised a brow, rocked back on his heels, and looked on with an expression both patronizing and puzzled as Coombes pulled a plastic shopping bag from his pocket, removed the book carefully from the table top, and placed it into the bag. 'I will be sure to give this back to you, sergeant,' said Coombes. 'I will take good care of it.'

'I can't imagine what you hope to learn from a book. It looks new.'

'Very new,' said Coombes. 'Now let us examine the area around the house. The rain of yesterday should have prepared the earth for tracks. A pity that the police have been driving in and out, tromping here and there.'

'We had to arrive, Mr Coombes,' said Bundle with a smile, and he held his finger in the air. 'We had to arrive, didn't we, sir?'

Coombes hopped down the front steps. He circled the cottage, looking carefully at the ground as he went, pausing every few paces to look up at the house, at the nearby trees, at the surrounding area. He then made his way along the driveway, staying to the edge. The driveway was light sand and gravel, damp with rain. Every once in a while I heard Coombes groan 'Ah!' as if he'd found something. When he reached the end of the drive he motioned me towards him and pointed to a patch of sand amidst grass at the very margin. 'Can you see the tracks – a fat bicycle tyre. What they call a mountain bike tyre.'

'I see it,' I said. 'Barely.'

'Let me call your attention to this other set of tracks, nearby. Two sets of bicycle tracks. One going in, one coming out. Both at the very edge of the driveway.'

'They become plainer and plainer as I stare.'

'Now look, Wilson, in the centre of the drive. Someone walked to the cottage in the rain last night. You see occasionally a footprint. Many of the prints have been wiped out by the tyre prints of police vehicles, but many remain.'

Coombes was off again, turning right at the end of the drive and proceeding along the edge of the lane, squatting so low that he seemed to be almost crawling. He darted along like a monkey, past Mrs Ogmore's driveway, and then he veered into the trees. Suddenly he stood and waved at me and shouted, 'Go get the car!'

I walked back to The Old Vicarage where Sergeant Bundle was waiting. We drove out into the lane, turned right, and then I spotted Coombes far into the trees, on his hands and knees.

'Lord, Lord, what is that man doing!' cried Bundle. 'I am responsible for him!'

Coombes crawled awhile, then suddenly stood and held
up what appeared to be a black cloth. He waved it at us
and then made his way towards the lane, on an angle. We
picked him up and drove on slowly.

'You crawled a long way through the grass, Mr Coombes,'
said Bundle. 'I've never seen detective work done in that
manner before.'

'It was necessary.'

'Ah, but you crawled a very long way for a man of your
age,' said Bundle. 'I don't know if that is good.'

'You mustn't take your duties too seriously, sergeant. I
found something of interest.'

'Yes?'

Coombes held up a black pillow slip.

'How very odd,' said Bundle. 'Who would sleep on black
sheets?'

'Fashion,' I said.

'Odder still,' said Coombes, 'is that two holes have been
cut in it – apparently eye holes.'

'Do you see a connection between this and the murder?'
asked Bundle.

'We must ponder that possibility,' said Coombes. He leant
back in his seat, closed his eyes, and pressed his fingers
together. He did not speak for the rest of the short journey.
But when we reached Chancery Lane Coombes said to
Bundle, 'By the way, sergeant, could *Lydia* be the girl's
name that the victim mentioned to Mr Twembley?'

'Yes, yes, that was it!' cried Bundle. '*Lydia*, yes. Where
did you see that name, sir?'

'Just a guess, Bundle, just a guess.'

That evening Coombes was much changed. He was no
longer depressed. He seemed alternately in a state of alert
agitation, meditative calm, and reflective melancholy.
He sat in front of the fire with his fingers pressed together,
staring into the flames or up at the ceiling. All at once
he sprang from his chair – as if he had been tied there and
suddenly burst his bonds – and he began to pace the floor
mercilessly, wall to wall, around and around. Suddenly he
stopped. A faraway look invaded his face. His shoulders

fell a little, as if an unwelcome thought had just overtaken him. He turned to me and said, 'Do you think they really need me on this case, Wilson? Or are Bundle and my Scotland Yard contact merely concocting therapy?'

'Therapy?' I said, looking up from my book.

'Therapy for an old man, yes.'

'I haven't the foggiest idea what you are talking about. Whatever can you mean, Coombes? You say the strangest things sometimes. I begin to wonder if you are keeping some deep dark secret from the world.'

'Perhaps I am, Wilson,' said he, in a faraway voice. 'Perhaps I am.'

'Who is this mysterious contact of yours at Scotland Yard? And what has he to do with Sergeant Bundle? Bundle is always referring to your famous contact – with a *wink wink*, and a *nod nod*. I am not a terribly clever man, Coombes, but I do pick up on the obvious.'

Coombes stalked back and forth across the floor with renewed anxiety, rubbing the back of his neck with his hand. 'Yes, yes, I doubt you could help me unless you knew all the facts.'

'I don't wish to pry into any man's secrets,' I said. 'But I have wondered why the police should be consulting *you* on a murder case. I've been baffled from the beginning. A common man such as me needs to be provided with a few facts before he can judge a matter.'

'Quite so, quite so.'

'If ever you wish to tell me what your connection is with this mysterious "Scotland Yard" contact, I'd be very glad to listen.'

For a moment he paused in front of the fire and seemed about to tell me something. Then he walked on, at a gentler pace, still rubbing his neck. 'It is a very long story, Watson . . .'

'Wilson.'

'I could hardly expect you to believe it even if I dared tell you.'

There we left it, for the time being.

FOUR
Suspicions of the Impossible

I did not sleep well that night. Coombes reminded me of someone. How very odd! More and more I had the feeling he was a person I had once known well – perhaps in Afghanistan, or in schooldays at Eton, or even back in the early days of childhood in my father's garden. The notion grew on me that Coombes had been not merely a remote acquaintance but someone I had been more or less intimately acquainted with. Stuff and nonsense! Impossible. Very odd, though. Perhaps I felt this way only because I was living in a retirement dream where nothing seemed entirely real, living in a town that was a fairy tale – a Kingdom of Books! I wandered through its crooked streets as if under a spell, navigating into tiny bookshops where I hoped to meet Mr Pickwick, or Miss Havisham, then prowling through a gloomy castle heaped with books so ruinously mouldy that I scarcely dared touch them for fear of being poisoned. I began to wonder if the horrors of Afghanistan were with me still, causing me to hallucinate.

I opened my eyes to a bright morning. As I shaved I could smell toast, tea. Coombes had been up for hours, apparently. I resisted the temptation to be the first to say *good morning*. I poured myself a cup of Earl Grey, sat down before the cold fire, and sipped.

Coombes was staring at the wall, evidently deep in contemplation. He appeared to spend half his life energetically gathering facts and details, the other half sitting in a stupor while processing those facts in his brain. I had to admit that I liked the man, cold and analytical as he was. He seemed to mean well. When he wasn't impatiently seeking out more facts, he was genial enough. When his strange, cold passions made him, for a moment, rude, he was always ready to see his fault and apologize. Yet his strange silences and occasional dramatic poses seemed at times to border on affectation. I found them annoying. I sipped the Earl Grey and made the slightest move to reach for my book, intending to go read it on the patio. But Coombes stopped me with a sudden cry. 'You know, Wilson, this case has some very singular features!'

'Horrible,' I said. 'A literal blood bath.'

'It has rejuvenated me enormously,' he said.

'I've noticed that,' I said, feeling a twinge of revulsion.

He sprang from his chair and almost sprinted to the window, hopping slightly on his injured leg. 'I wish I had a pipe,' he said.

'If you smoke I'll be obliged to move out,' I said.

'Oh, I shan't smoke ever again. My London doctor strictly prohibits it and I wouldn't wish to disappoint him after he has worked so hard. I have an appointment with him next week, and he would find me out.' Coombes laughed.

'I thought you had an appointment with him just a few weeks ago. Are you ill, Coombes?'

'Not ill – though I ought to be. I feel perfectly healthy, apart from my injured leg, but he has good reasons for wishing to check on me once a month.'

I let this cryptic statement pass. I stood up and poured another cup of tea. 'Well, tell me, Coombes, have you cracked the case for Sergeant Bundle?'

'Not *cracked* it, I'm afraid, though the general outlines of the crime are clear enough.'

'Well, I'm certain Sergeant Bundle will be happy to hear any theory you may have,' I said. 'He appeared to be completely at sea.'

'Ah, poor Bundle. He is one of those blustering, ambitious sorts who grabs on to things with great gusto and heaves each detail, willy-nilly, into the scales of judgement. But as he does so he is apt to drop facts and crush evidence and inadvertently leave his thumb on the scale as he weighs the evidence. He has not the delicacy of touch or refinement of mind to nudge the truth out of trifles. He is boisterous and willing, but lacks true talent.'

It was just this sort of supercilious comment that some-times rubbed me the wrong way and made me wonder what sort of man Coombes really was. 'Come, now, Coombes. The man was doing his job. I rather like him.'

'He is a splendid fellow,' said Coombes. 'He has a big heart and he does his best. I would even go so far as to say that in certain crude situations he is just the man who can . . . well, speak of the Devil.'

A uniformed blur appeared beyond the whorled leaded panes of our sitting room. A moment later Sergeant Bundle filled the small doorway, loomed into the room, and joined us for tea.

'Just a wee cup,' said he, rubbing his hands together. 'And then I must be on my way. Mr Coombes, I have come for the book. The crime lab wishes to take prints from the cover – I know you have been very careful with it.'

'Very careful,' said Coombes. 'I have kept my prints off of it.'

'We are thorough, Mr Coombes. Our department is small, but thorough. It is my belief that the book was owned by Mr Jenkins. His whole house is full of books. It is unusual that a murderer would bring reading material to a crime.' Bundle laughed, and took a sip.

'In this case the murderer did,' said Coombes.

The smile fell off of Bundle's face. 'Do you think so, sir?'

'I have a theory that may interest you,' said Coombes, coolly.

'Ah, theories are well, theories are good,' said Bundle, his optimism and self-confidence instantly returning. 'Theories always interest me. But in the end what we need are practical results, Mr Coombes. Practical results – that is what our citizens always crave and cry for.'

'Sometimes theories lead to practical results,' said Coombes.

'Books seldom provide much evidence at crime scenes,' said Bundle. 'That's my theory. That is why I ignored that book.'

'I'm afraid you were right,' said Coombes. 'The book disappointed me.'

Bundle laughed, gesturing with a thick and rosy hand. 'Well, there you are, sir,' he said.

'Still, my research into the book has not proved entirely barren,' said Coombes.

'Did it reveal something?' asked Bundle sceptically, curiously, nervously, raising a large bushy eyebrow.

'Not as much as I had hoped,' said Coombes.

Bundle grinned. 'Well, I thought as much.'

'It only revealed,' said Holmes, 'that the murderer is an actor with dark hair who very likely has lived in Afghanistan, spent his youthful years in North America, received his later education in England, and now lives in or near London. The book also suggests that he travelled from London to Hay-on-Wye by train and by bus, that he made this journey sometime since last Saturday, that he is methodical, highly educated, despises the present US Government of George W. Bush, and probably owns a very distinctive automobile – perhaps a vintage car.'

'My heavens!' cried Bundle. 'Did he write his entire life story in the margins?'

'He wrote two brief marginal notes, commenting on the text.'

Glancing over Coombes's shoulder I saw that the book was titled *Abu Ghraib: Torture and Betrayal*. On the cover was that famous picture – that all the world has seen and that has brought such discredit upon the United States of America – of a man standing awkwardly on a stool of some sort, wearing a black robe and a black hood, with wires attached to his body, as he is being tortured by US troops.

The picture aroused all my memories of the war, and a cold bolt of fear shot through my heart, surprising me. I was almost trembling. 'My God, Coombes!' I murmured. 'Then here is the significance of the black hood you found in the bushes . . .'

'Exactly!' cried Coombes, and his eyes flashed.

'What do you mean?' asked Bundle.

Out of a plastic shopping bag by his chair Coombes pulled the black hood made from a pillow slip. 'I have examined this,' he said, 'and found in it two hairs that match the strand of hair I found in the book. Also, actor's pancake make-up smeared on the inside of this hood will, I suspect, match smears of make-up that can be detected on pages thirty-eight and two hundred and thirteen of the book. Evidently on two occasions he inadvertently touched his face before turning a page.'

'I cannot imagine how you deduced all of these things from a book,' said Bundle, looking earnest, bewildered, and slightly defeated.

'A cursory and quite superficial glance at the book reveals all I have mentioned,' said Coombes. 'That the man is an actor is suggested not only by the pancake make-up and the dramatic manner in which the crime was carried out, but by the fact that both of the pencilled marginal notes refer to the theatre. The first of these notes is a simple transcription of poetry from *The Merchant of Venice*. In the empty space at the end of chapter three he has pencilled the famous passage beginning "The quality of mercy is not strain'd,/ It droppeth as the gentle rain from heaven/Upon the place beneath: it is twice bless'd:" and so on. Anyone can memorize poetry, but this man goes on quoting for nineteen lines. Indeed, I am almost inclined to think he has played a part in that play. To quote at such length suggests a man in love with the language of the theatre, and unable to stop before he has finished the cadence.

'The second marginal note is truly in a margin, next to a paragraph discussing the role of George W. Bush in beginning a war which has resulted in the death of as many as six hundred thousand Iraqis. The note reads thus: *He might play Macbeth if he could but speak the lines without stumbling. Death colours all his acts, and his only defence is ignorance.*

'That the murderer is a male is suggested by the handwriting, which is elegant but assertive. The style, on the whole, is an American style of handwriting, yet the spelling is British. The word *colour*, for instance, is not spelled with a *u* in America, and *defence* with a *c* is British usage. This suggests that he first learnt cursive handwriting as a child while living in North America, and that he spent his later

years in Britain, or at least somewhere in the British Empire.
That he also was educated in Afghanistan is suggested by
the impress of four words on the back of the dust jacket,
as if he had used the book for a support as he wrote something on another sheet of paper. Those words are in Pashto,
the primary language of Afghanistan. It is true that Pashto
is also spoken in some other countries, but to a much lesser
extent. More might be learnt by translating the words, which
I cannot do.

'That the book was purchased at Hatchards in Piccadilly
is indicated by the bookseller's cash receipt that I found
tucked between two pages in the middle of the book. The
receipt indicates the book was bought last Saturday. That
it was bought no earlier than last Saturday I also know
because I telephoned the store and learnt that that is the
first date they sold it. I was aware it was only recently
published because I have been looking forward to its appearance in the bookstores myself.

'That he rode the train from London is suggested by the
long handwritten passage from Shakespeare. It begins
fluently written but ends in a jiggle of letters. Evidently he
began writing at a station stop but before he could complete
the passage the train resumed its journey, and consequently
the letters of the last half of the passage are spidery and
hard to read. Towards the end of the book I found a small
strip of paper used as a bookmark, obviously torn out of
some publication. In fact, it was torn from the Hereford-
London train schedule. I have a copy of that schedule here
in my pocket, in anticipation of my journey to London next
week to see my doctor. The several lines of print visible
on the bookmark scrap exactly match those on the last page
of my schedule.

'The bus ride is only an educated guess. The bus is the
usual mode of public transport for most who travel by train
to Hereford and must journey on to Hay. He might have
hired a taxi, but I think that unlikely. He has gone to great
lengths to remain anonymous and unremarked, and would
not wish a taxi driver to remember him. He might even
have ridden a bicycle from Hereford. I have wondered why

he did not drive to Wales. It occurred to me that either he had no car, or had a car that was too easily remembered. He wouldn't wish to rent a car, for that would be a matter of record. By contrast, a train journey is an anonymous journey.'

Sergeant Bundle looked both stunned and pleased. He was shaking his head, almost in amusement.

I felt stunned and not pleased. A terrible sense of *déjà vu* had come over me again. I wondered – with a strange sinking feeling in my heart – *where have I heard all this before?*

'It sounds as if we are well on the way to solving this case, sir,' opined Bundle, swelling in his chair and taking a deep breath.

'I wish I could be so optimistic,' said Coombes.

'Have you further theories?' asked Bundle. 'I should be very glad to hear them.'

Coombes sprang from his chair and hobbled to the window, then turned and faced Bundle. 'I think you will learn that young Mr Calvin Hawes was recently a military man with the American forces.'

'You are right, sir!' cried Bundle. 'We have already learnt that he served as an infantryman with the American army in Afghanistan, and was discharged a year ago.'

'I believe you will find he was lured to Hay-on-Wye by the promise that a young woman was awaiting him here. No doubt he thought her name was *Lydia Languish*.'

Bundle nodded. 'The bouquet in the poor lad's hands, is that it? It seems most probable.'

'Few things are more potent to a young man than the promise of sex,' said Coombes. 'Even money pales in comparison. What better to lure him all the way across an ocean? Attraction to women is not a sensation I have personally experienced, yet I have observed that for most men it is an overpowering madness. Young men in particular.'

'Very true, sir.'

'If you succeed in breaking into his email you may well find that he was corresponding, or thought he was corresponding, with Lydia Languish. I don't know how computers work, but I suspect the murderer does, and that he has covered his computer tracks better than he covered his bicycle tracks. So you are unlikely to track him down in that manner. You might, however, enquire of bicycle shops here and in Hereford to learn whether they have in the past week sold a bicycle that leaves tracks like these . . .' Coombes handed the sergeant a small print of a photograph.

'I didn't know you had a computer!' I said. 'You astonish me, Coombes.'

'One must keep up with the times – difficult as it is to do.'

'Well, *tempus fugit*, Mr Coombes. I must be off and running,' said Bundle. He rose from his chair, and seemed to fill the room. His white shirt and tie, and the epaulettes on his shirt, made him look very grand.

A moment later he was gone.

'Come, Wilson. I must show you my computer. A very strange little thing it is.' He led me up the stairs to his room.

'I had no idea you had so many books up here too!' I cried, for they were ranged on shelves all round the room, and piled in corners. On the desk was a new laptop computer, and on the side table a small colour printer.

'Certain friends have outfitted me with all the latest machinery,' said he. 'I have found the computer somewhat more convenient than notebooks for storing information – although for field work a notebook is indispensable.'

'And what, may I ask, is the object of your researches? I have often wondered but been reluctant to ask.'

'Reluctance to ask is a very English fault, my dear fellow. But there is no secret. I am trying to catch up with what I've missed.'

'It is something I ought to do myself,' I said. 'Much of life has slid by me unnoticed. Now that I have leisure, I want to try to catch up on what I've ignored before. But what exactly are you trying to catch up on?'

'Everything,' said Coombes, and suddenly he looked a bit deflated. 'And it is a Herculean task.'

'If you try to catch up on everything, I imagine it would be,' I said.

'I must away to work, Wilson!' he cried, seeming to gather his energy again. He began grabbing volumes from the wall.

I went downstairs, finished my tea, ate a biscuit, then wandered into the street and up towards the centre of town, feeling more lost than I had felt in many a year. I scarcely know what I did that day, perambulating through crooked streets, into and out of bookshops, rambling in the hills, then back into town, filled with half-formed decisions, musings, uncertainty. I ate my evening meal at a restaurant, then walked to Cambrai Cottage. Coombes was seated in front of a roaring fire. 'Greetings, Wilson!' said he, in a cheery voice.

'Good evening, Coombes – very chilly weather.'

'Chilly indeed,' said he, and he rubbed his hands together and looked into the flames.

I set the books I had purchased on the table, five lovely volumes bound in full green morocco. I carefully placed them so that their gilt titles were in plain view of my strange acquaintance. After a few minutes I saw Coombes glance towards them. But he did not display much interest.

I wandered to one end of the room, gazed out the window. I turned, considered making a pot of tea. Coombes seemed deep in meditation. His back was to me and he was staring towards the mantelpiece. I felt in the pockets of my sport coat, contemplating my next move. It suddenly seemed to me that I may have been wrong to buy the Sherlock Holmes volumes merely to try a foolish experiment, and that I should really have spent my money on . . .

'You are absolutely right, Wilson, you *should* have bought *The Pickwick Papers*,' said Coombes, 'and you will regret it if you do not go to Boz Books and buy it before someone else does.'

I froze. He had broken in on my mental processes. He had replied to my unspoken thought. A thrill of coldness ran through me. I knew where I had seen this trick before. 'Ye gods!' I cried, walking round to where I could face him. 'That is just what I was thinking. But how in the world did you know it? I think you really must be Sherlock Holmes! Or else I'm losing my mind—'

'Elementary, my dear Wilson.'

'I *am* losing my mind,' I said, and I sank into a chair with my head in my hand. 'This is some sort of giant charade, to which I have fallen victim.'

'Nothing of the kind,' said Coombes. 'All this while that you thought I was staring and vacantly contemplating, I was in fact watching you in that mirror by the mantle. I saw you place those Sherlock Holmes volumes on the table, in hopes that they would cause some sort of reaction in me. You carefully angled the books so I could see the titles. When I did not react as you had hoped, you gazed at your newly purchased books ruefully, then turned away and walked to the window. Then you turned back into the room again as if uncertain or upset. You looked again at the set of books you had just bought, and then you looked down at the Boz Books pamphlet protruding so flamboyantly from the pocket of your jacket, and you gave a deep sigh. Your train of thought was obvious: you were thinking that instead of buying the set of Sherlock Holmes you should have purchased the first edition of *Pickwick Papers* that you have so often mentioned. You have often said that a *Pickwick* with both of the cancelled Buss plates is a rare find, and that you will never get it at a better price.'

I stared like a man bereft of his wits.

'There is hardly anything at all in my observation,' he added. 'You have been mentioning that *Pickwick Papers* volume so frequently in the last ten days that anyone could have guessed your thought.'

'But I have seen this done before only by one person,' I said. 'You even look like him. For weeks I have been trying to remember where I have seen you before, and now it has come upon me. And yet it cannot be so!'

'It was inevitable that you would discover me,' he said. 'I have seen it coming for a long time. And I have feared it, Wilson . . . I have feared it a little.'

'What is it you have feared, Coombes?'

'I have feared you would find out who I am.'

'And who are you?'

'Since you have become my friend, I might as well confess,' he said. 'Anyway, you already know.'

'Know what?' I said, trying to project a manly voice. But the words came out almost a whisper.

'It is too late at night for confessions,' said Coombes. 'Tomorrow morning, if you still desire it, I will tell you everything.'

That night I again slept fitfully, wondering what strange tale I might hear in the morning. I arose early but Coombes had arisen earlier. He was already shaved and dressed. We went out to breakfast together and only chatted on commonplace topics – the quality of food in England versus food on the continent, Welsh myths in relation to Greek myths, and whether the notion that ontogeny recapitulates phylogeny might apply to psychic development. But when we returned to our cottage the subject could be avoided no longer. I stoked the fire. My friend leant back and, placing his elbows on the arms of the chair, he touched all his finger and thumb tips together and gazed at me steadily, with a kindly and curious gaze. 'I have seen you struggling with this problem for weeks, and now you have guessed, and guessed correctly, my dear Watson . . .'

'Wilson.'

'. . . that I am Sherlock Holmes.'

'Sherlock Holmes!' I murmured.

'Is not that what you have been thinking?'

'Yes – but that's impossible!'

'Improbable, certainly. But as a man of science I am not terribly surprised that good Dr Coleman of St Bartholomew's Hospital, with the help of his many able assistants and all his modern equipment, has been able to bring me back to life – presuming, of course, that I was actually dead . . . a point upon which the metaphysicians of the scientific fraternity seem unable to agree.'

A fit of nervousness came over me. My hands were actually trembling. I arose and walked to the window. I gazed out at the commonplace and comforting street. I gazed a long while. At last I said, 'You are a very good actor, sir.'

Coombes ignored my evasions. 'Awakening my brain was

relatively easy, they tell me. But bringing my body back to function, after ninety years lying frozen in a glacier, was a long, complicated and painful ordeal – indeed, I am not at all sure I would have gone through it if they had given me a choice. But of course I had no choice.'

'A glacier!' I cried.

'Perhaps I should begin at the beginning,' said Coombes, with equanimity. 'I take it from the look of horrified disbelief on your face that you are interested.'

'Yes,' I said, and I sank into my chair. I had no intention of believing whatever it was he had to tell. But I was certainly interested. Here is what he told me. As he spoke he seemed to intoxicate me, and – for some moments at least – I became quite certain that it was really the voice of Sherlock Holmes speaking . . .

FIVE

Cedric Coombes and Sherlock Holmes

I must go back a bit and refresh your memory of history, Wilson, if you are to understand the strange adventure that befell me in the year 1914. The Great War, as I'm sure you recall from your history books, was precipitated when Archduke Franz Ferdinand of Austria-Hungary visited Sarajevo, the capital of Bosnia, and was assassinated by a Serbian fanatic. In retaliation, Austria-Hungary declared war on tiny Serbia, and soon was backed up by its ally, Germany. Russia, in defence of its fellow Slavs in Serbia, jumped in and declared war on both Germany and Austria-Hungary. Britain and France were added to the mix, simply because they had, for many years, been loosely united with Russia. So Russia, France and Great Britain aligned themselves against the Triple Alliance of Germany, Austria-Hungary and Italy. Thus the stage was set for war. All the props were in place. All the actors were dressed up in soldiers' uniforms and waiting in the wings, ready to unleash death on a scale never before witnessed in this world.

Many people tried to prevent the conflict. The three people best placed to do this were Kaiser Wilhelm II of Germany, King George V of England, and Czar Nicholas II of Russia. The first two, George and Wilhelm, were grandchildren of Queen Victoria, which made them first cousins. Nicholas was married to one of Victoria's grandchildren, which made him a sort of first cousin by marriage. The assassination of Ferdinand took place on June 28th. During the month of July few people seriously believed that war would break out. But great forces were gathering, and the three cousins sensed that a juggernaut may have been set in motion. Telegrams flew back and forth between them. They had been children and young men together, and they often signed themselves *Nicky, Willy* and *Georgie* when they wrote to each other. But all this flurry of telegraphic conversation between the cousins was to no avail. Britain followed its allies and declared war on August 4th, 1914.

Now, if you recall my own history, as transcribed by my old friend Watson, you will know that in 1912 I had come out of retirement to track down a German spy named Von Bork. The task took two years. On August 2nd, 1914, I finally collared Von Bork and, with the help of my friend Watson, trussed him like a turkey, loaded him into a motorcar and carried him off to Scotland Yard.

I immediately returned to Sussex, intending to resume my quiet life of retirement. But scarcely had I arrived home when Britain declared war. Soon I began to chafe that I was no longer able to help the cause of England. I was a man of sixty, but I was perfectly fit in both body and mind. I wondered how I might make shift to assist my country in this terrible moment. The answer was not long in coming. A messenger rode up my cottage lane one morning, leant his bicycle against the low wall, and handed me a letter from our King. It was dated from Buckingham Palace and was signed by the King himself. Prime Minister Asquith had visited me in my cottage two years earlier, imploring my assistance on the Von Bork case. Now the King was requesting that I come to Buckingham Palace to discuss 'a matter of grave national importance.'

I travelled to London the following day and was met at London Bridge Station by a representative from Buckingham Palace, a portly gentleman who introduced himself as Earnest Hobbes. Hobbes escorted me to a motorcar driven by an intense young gentleman who had a scar on his cheek and never spoke. This young chauffeur bowed punctiliously after the German manner. 'I observe,' I said, 'that you have attended Heidelberg University, where I once visited Professor Grundauer. Do you know him?' To my surprise, the chauffeur looked almost frightened. He bowed again, took my valise and set it in the boot. He lunged into the driver's seat and drove us to Claridges Hotel in Brook Street, where my room had been arranged.

The following day a carriage and four arrived to carry me to the palace. October 20th it was, a crisp autumn day, a Tuesday. Purple clouds tumbled through the sky like little icebergs, and red leaves tumbled across roads, and ladies held on to their hats. The driver took the broad streets through Grosvenor Square over to Park Lane and south to Piccadilly, then into Constitution Hill and so to Buckingham Palace. I entered the Palace and a gentleman took my coat. Another gentleman led me upstairs to the White Drawing Room. He led me to the far left-hand corner of the room, straight to a cabinet surmounted by a massive mirror. He touched something and the cabinet and mirror swung open intact, giving us direct access to The Royal Closet. The time was precisely two o'clock. Barely had my eyes adjusted to the muted light when I became aware of someone slipping through the side door that led to The Throne Room. I heard the door close with a muffled thud. I felt suddenly hermetically sealed, as if in a laboratory vessel. In an instant the King stood before me looking very relaxed despite the stiff white tunic he wore. His full moustache and beard looked better up close than in pictures, and they flowed into each other so that his mouth seemed to have a life of its own when he kindly greeted me. 'Good day, Mr Holmes, so good of you to come,' he said. He was a fine looking man and might have been more impressive had it not been for slightly bulging eyes that gave him a look of perpetual surprise. He was exquisitely gracious, humble and firm as he explained to me the importance of what he was asking me to do. The lives of hundreds of thousands of people, he said, were in the balance. He was asking me to help save perhaps a whole generation of young Frenchmen, Englishmen, Germans and Russians by carrying to the Kaiser a last appeal and final plan to end the conflict.

At that moment came a knock, and the door opened slightly and someone handed the King a small leather case. 'Thank you,' he said, and the door clicked closed, sealing

us up once more as if we were in a tomb. That image
occurred to me. With a hurried step he came towards me
and set the case on an ornate table. The case was small,
made of stitched camel-coloured leather. It had two brass
catches with a lock between them. It was similar to what
is now called an *attaché* case.

'I want you to take this to Kaiser Wilhelm, my cousin,'
he said.

'I have met the Kaiser,' I said.

'That is one reason why I particularly need you to undertake this mission,' said the King. 'Cousin Willy knows you,
and he is indebted to you for having helped his family avoid
disgrace on that previous unfortunate occasion. He will open
his door to you . . . if you can but reach him.'

'If I may ask, sir,' said I, 'why do you not send the case
through normal diplomatic channels?'

'Simply put,' replied the King, 'I do not trust many people
any more. These are far from normal times, Mr Holmes,
and people change as times change. The guns have been
roaring for more than two months, battles have been fought,
and there are many men who, although in July they tried
to prevent the conflict, now have no interest in stopping it,
feeling that victory will be theirs. To be candid, Mr Holmes,
I no longer trust Ambassador Lichnowsky or his staff to
see that my messages are delivered to their Kaiser. In truth,
I no longer trust – in the deepest sense of that word – even
some of my own staff. Therefore I ask for your help. I know
your reputation, Holmes. I know that if you *say* you will
do a thing, you will do it. I trust not only your discretion
but your talent. If the thing can be done, I believe you can
do it. And if you tell me you will try, I believe no man on
earth will try more tenaciously. But I warn you, sir, it will
be a most difficult and dangerous mission.'

'I hope,' I replied, 'I am not immodest when I say that
difficulty inspires me, and that danger has always been my
companion.'

'Then you will undertake the journey?' he asked.

'It will be my honour to do so,' I replied.

'Thank you, Mr Holmes.' He shook my hand. Then he

touched the case, laid it on its side, stroked it absently with his hand. 'This case is locked, Mr Holmes, and it must never be opened by anyone but the Kaiser himself.' The King held out a key and laid it on the case. I took it and pocketed it.

'It contains,' said the King, 'documents recalling our childhood, which I hope may make Willy reminisce and put him in a trusting mood. It also contains documents outlining a plan for ending the conflict and for rewarding Willy if he helps me end it. And, finally, it contains a letter challenging Willy to be daring with me in making this one last desperate dash for peace.'

We spoke then of the journey I was about to undertake, of the best routes for skirting the line of battle and entering Germany. He handed me a pouch containing money and travelling papers. Again someone knocked on the door. The King hastened to open it, said something to someone, returned to me. He explained to me that he was leaving Buckingham Palace in an hour. The affairs of state so pressed on him, he said, that he needed to get away for a few days and relax a little, but always in the last minutes before his departure there were people clamouring to catch him before he vanished. He did not wish to rush our conversation, however. It was, he said, a conversation as important as any he had had in his life. We spoke a little while longer, then shook hands again.

Suddenly he vanished, and it was over. I stepped out of the room. I was led downstairs. The gentleman who had taken my coat now presented it back to me, and helped me into it. I walked past the guards towards a black carriage with four huge white horses at the ready. I climbed briskly inside the carriage and settled myself. A clattering of hooves, the gentle rattle and creak, the smell of leather. I felt a pleasurable rush of anticipation, the same I always feel when a great adventure is about to begin.

But even as we joggled through the great Buckingham Gate I sensed my adventure had already begun, for I noticed amidst the crowd on the pavement a tall man in a top hat who looked at my carriage most strangely. A few yards

later my eye fastened on a youth who gazed at me through
my carriage window. His dark eyes met mine only for an
instant, but there was something strange in his glance. The
youth wore black trousers, a shabby cloth coat . . . and new
military boots. The great beasts began to clatter in different
rhythm and the carriage swayed as we turned left and picked
up speed. We spun up Constitution Hill. Already some vague
tension told me it would be unwise for me to stay this night
at Claridges.

I must pause, dear Wilson, to explain something that
you, having been born in the age of the motor, may not
quite appreciate. For centuries the roads on every continent were ruled by horses. But in London, beginning about
1912 (as I recall), suddenly the roads began to play host
to a number of vehicles powered by motors. You would
look down a road and see an old horse-drawn omnibus
side by side with an identical two-storey omnibus powered
by a motor. The motorized versions looked very odd, at
first. They looked lacking, like an omnibus whose team
had run off. And I can tell you that these new motor
versions aroused at first a measure of antagonism. For
one thing, as more and more motor vehicles mingled with
horse-drawn vehicles, confusion ensued. Look down a
major artery and you would see two horsemen trotting
along, a motorcar wheezing behind them, a hansom cab
springing along past a motor-powered omnibus, a four-
wheel wagon pulled by a horse, a bicyclist speeding by
a crowd of lady pedestrians with parasols, and so on. As
you may imagine, accidents were common.

Such was the sort of confusion we encountered as we
boomed up Constitution Hill between the greenery of the
Palace Gardens on our left and the trees of Green Park on
our right. I sat alone on the right-hand side of the carriage
looking out the window. Suddenly I saw a 'four-wheeler'
cab veer crazily and overturn just ahead of us . . . a wheel
came off. The cab horse began to fight to get out of the
tangle of harness. The driver was thrown clear. A motorcar
came to a halt in front of our carriage, blocking us. We
lurched to a stop. A moment later a fight broke out, evidently

between the cab driver and the motorcar driver. The two men were brawling and howling all the vilest language. Suddenly one of them was thrown up against the side of our carriage. He slammed hard into the door beside me. I gazed down at him, saw his hat tumble into the dust, yet I could see he was not really hurt and was almost smiling. Then I sensed that the door on the other side of the carriage had opened. Turning, I saw an arm in a threadbare wool coat sleeve reaching into the carriage . . . but then the thief was snatched away by our guard, who had leapt off the box. The guard struggled briefly with the thief, but the thief squirmed, hit the guard, escaped. Instantly the guard leapt back up on to his seat by the driver. The driver shouted, the great horses whinnied, the carriage lurched ahead, I was thrown to the side . . . my eyes glanced down and I saw something amazing: on the floor beside me were two camel-coloured leather cases. Identical.

In a flash I understood what had happened. The whole elaborately staged scene played back through my brain. The perpetrators had timed their attack nearly perfectly, but not quite. Although the youth had managed to insert the duplicate case into the carriage, he had not managed to grab the original – for just at that point the guard had leapt on him. As the young man had struggled to break free I had heard him cry out a single word in Russian – not a polite word. Then he had run into Green Park and vanished.

Our carriage accelerated with the power of four great horses. Motor vehicles, carriages, wagons and pedestrians scattered as they saw us coming. We reached Park Lane and resumed the normal dignified pace. I was delivered to the door of Claridges without further difficulty.

I now had in my possession two identical cases. And I didn't know which was which. Usually I am a keen observer, but in the haste and hurry of leaving the King and mounting the carriage and being spirited away into the streets of London, I had not had time to examine the King's case closely. If I had, undoubtedly I would have noticed small points that would have allowed me to distinguish it. What to do? It occurred to me that I might return to Buckingham Palace and ask the King to open the two cases. Trouble was, the King was on his way somewhere and probably had already left. Then too, one hates to trouble a king. I decided my best course was to deliver the two cases to the Kaiser, explaining to him that one was false, the other true. It was plain to me that he would easily discern the one from the other, particularly since the true case included documents relating to the Kaiser's childhood.

When I reached my room at Claridges I realized I had lost one of my gloves. I knew it had been in my pocket when I had entered Buckingham Palace . . . the loss seemed minor. Other matters pressed on my mind, most especially escaping Claridges unseen and finding a safe place to stay the night. Hastily I put on face make-up and false eyebrows to make me look fifteen years older. I packed the two camel-coloured leather cases into my old travelling valise, along with my clothes, disguises and Webley service revolver. I jerked a sheet off the bed and spread it on the floor, then lay my valise and a wadded blanket in the middle of it. I gathered the four corners and made the sheet into a beggar's sack, tying the corners in a knot. Carrying my sack over my shoulder, I crept into the hallway and shuffled along, stooped, looking furtive. Soon one of the hotel staff accosted me indignantly, questioned me angrily, and threw me bodily into the dusky autumn street.

A sliver of white moon hung like a needle on the sky. As I limped away with the painful gait of a cripple, I peered from beneath my false brows to see who might be lingering near the hotel. A woman with a parasol held a tiny white poodle on a leash – the creature barked at me as I passed. A number of carriages were lined up along the kerb, their uniformed drivers lounging nearby. A tall man in a long coat stood beneath a tree, smoking a cigar. A boy ran shouting. A huge, bearlike bald man with a handlebar moustache knelt by the axle of a wagon and strained to replace the wheel. A Bobby stood near him, lifting an arm and urging him to hurry his task and get out of the traffic.

I hobbled north across Oxford Street, pulling off my false eyebrows and wiping the make-up off my face. I intended to throw off my disguise at the first opportunity and find a small hotel where I could stay the night, but suddenly I realized that my old lodgings at 221B Baker Street were quite near. I wondered whether Mrs Hudson might still live there, and whether she might, just possibly, lend me her spare room. Worth a try. I crossed the edge of Portman Square, passed into Baker Street and soon I was at the old familiar front door, which was just exactly as I had remembered it, although it wanted paint. I knocked, waited, and by and by the door opened a crack and a shrivelled face appeared. 'Mr Holmes!' she said. 'Why are you prowling about in that get-up? Oh, do come in, do come in!'

'Good evening, Mrs Hudson,' said I. 'You look as bright as you always did, though a little thinner.'

'I am frail but energetic,' she proclaimed.

Her struggling old figure preceded me up the stairs, and she tossed words over her shoulder as she explained, in an excited voice, that she had someone she wanted me to meet. 'You will be very glad to see him, Mr Holmes!' she said.

Could Watson have returned and be living again at 221B? Impossible!

She knocked on the door of my old apartments. When the door opened I gazed upon a complete stranger. I did not recognize the man at all. He was a robust fellow in his early forties, with a hearty manner and a long, smiling face.

'Mr Holmes,' he cried when he saw me, and his eyes lit up with surprise and joy. 'What are you doing prowling about in that get-up!' And then, to my astonishment, this stranger stepped forward and grabbed me, and he hugged me. I was like a doll in his powerful arms. Then he pushed me away and held me at arm's length, held me by the shoulders, and he shook me a little, and he said, 'How very good to look upon your face again, sir! You have not changed at all!'

I was utterly bewildered.

The man laughed. 'Can it be that you, the famous Sherlock Holmes who can discern, at a single glance, the complete

life history of a complete stranger – can it be that you
cannot recognize your old colleague in crime detection! It
is I, sir! It is Willie Wiggins, the captain of your Baker
Street Irregulars!'

'Wiggins,' I cried. I peered. Then, slowly, I recognized
the boyish face of young Willie Wiggins behind the mature
face that was before me. 'My heavens! You've grown up!'

'I had no choice, sir,' said he. 'I had no choice.'

Willie and his wife, the dark woman who appeared behind
him in the doorway, invited me in and introduced me to
their two young children. Mrs Hudson cooked us supper
that night, and dined with us. Over a joint of beef and roast
potatoes I learnt that Willie was now a manager of the
Southeast and Chatham Railway. The reason he lived in
this apartment was that it was the only home he'd ever
known or aspired to. I had never had any idea that my
humble lodgings had appeared so grand in his childish
imagination. He told me that Alfie Berk – Willie's lieutenant
in the Irregulars back in '81 – was now a police detective
on the metropolitan force. According to Willie, Alfie always
proclaimed that he had started out as a detective at the age
of seven and he saw no advantage in learning a new trade.
Dougie Duggin, did I remember him? Yes, yes I did. The
little boy with the exuberant spirit and the fat face and torn
ear. Dougie was dead, killed in a tavern brawl in Deptford.
He had turned to burglary, went bad to worse, and at the
end Willie had never seen him anything but drunk.

After supper, Willie and his wife Thelma turned their
children out of the children's own bedroom, which once
had been my bedroom. They insisted I sleep there for the
night while the young ones took the couch. I am not a
terribly warm person, Wilson, but I felt very warm that
night – warmer than I have felt in the past ninety years,
that is sure! Lying beneath that old ceiling, with all its old
cracks in the same old places, and hearing horses occasionally passing on the street as they did of old, and thinking
of times I had spent in that room musing on crimes long
solved and forgotten, I could not help but think of old
Watson and the excitements that had sprung upon us in this

old house – and how he and I were once young and now
suddenly were becoming old men. I stared at the old ceiling
and I felt the nostalgia and miracle and sadness of passing
time more poignantly than ever I had before, or ever I have
since. I think I may never again feel such a keen sense of
loss as I did that night in that old house in my old bedroom,
not if I should live a thousand years. It was all real, and
close, and warm, and vanishing. Forever vanishing as I fell
asleep.

Next morning, as the first beams of sunlight warmed the
bricks and trees and pavements of Baker Street, Willie
Wiggins looked out the front window and informed me that
the house was being watched by three men. One was burly,
bald, bearlike, with a handlebar moustache. He held a shovel
and was pretending to repair the paving stones. Another
was tall and slim and faced away from the house while
holding a small spy mirror in the fold of his newspaper.
The third was a stocky redheaded individual who leant
against a tree and held a cup of something hot. Willie
reported that he also saw a new motorized omnibus, a line
of three motorcars, two hansom cabs, a tradesman's wagon,
two bicyclists, a woman walking a tiny white poodle, a man
sitting on a blanket playing a flute, and two mothers pushing
prams. One of the mothers glanced up at Willie from moment
to moment – but that, said Willie, was the surest sign she
was a normal passerby. 'Normal women cannot help gazing
at me,' said he.

'Oh, Willie!' said his wife.

He laughed.

I told Willie that I needed to catch the earliest possible
train to France. Most of all, I needed to get away from the
house without being seen.

'That should not be difficult,' said Willie. 'I have an old
trunk.'

An hour later Willie and his friend from next door loaded
Willie's old steamship trunk on to a tradesman's cart parked
in front of the house. I felt cramped inside, but I could breathe
easily enough. As the horse plodded away with me I noticed
(through the keyhole) that the big bald man who had been

fixing the paving stones had vanished, leaving his shovel fallen against a fence. On my slow ride to Charing Cross I closed my eyes and listened to the voices of Willie and the wagon driver speculating about when the war would end. I listened to sounds of horses clopping and whinnying, squawky horns, clatter of wheels, rattle of harness, swish of tires, footfalls on pavement, shouts of drivers, hum and wheeze of motors, voices of people surging and fading. Every once in a while I heard a dog barking excitedly.

At Charing Cross Station Willie used his influence to see that the trunk was loaded into a locked baggage car. He spoke through the lid: 'The warning signs are up in the station, Mr Holmes – a very rough crossing in the Channel.'

'Not to worry,' I whispered.

'It won't be long now and I'll have you out of there,' said Willie.

By and by I felt gentle motion as the train began to roll. Shortly Willie undid the hasp and opened the lid and I climbed out.

We sat together on the trunk lid and looked out the window: steam flew by, trees whizzed, brown countryside jiggled in the distance. We talked all the way to Canterbury, and as we talked William Wiggins, district manager for the Southeast and Chatham Railway, slowly turned into little Willie Wiggins of the Baker Street Irregulars. More and more I could see little Willie Wiggins in the train manager's gestures and expressions. He told me over and over that I looked the same as he'd remembered. 'The way you're going, you'll last another hundred years,' said Willie.

'I hope not,' said I.

Little did we know.

The train stopped at Chatham, then Canterbury. I began to feel pleased. Soon I would be boarding the boat at Dover. Once I had reached the continent unobserved, it would be nearly impossible for anyone to pursue me. I mentioned this to Willie as we sat in the Canterbury station. Scarcely had I done so when I heard a tapping, then a banging.

'Somebody is breaking into this car!' whispered Willie.

We darted into the shadows behind a pile of luggage.

Now came a loud cracking sound. The door opened and a huge bald man with a handlebar moustache lunged up into the car and rushed to the trunk in which I had been hidden. He held an iron crowbar high over his head with his right hand as he leant down and flung open the trunk lid with his left hand. He stared into blackness, stupefied: 'Was ist den dass!' he cried in amazement. He gazed down into emptiness.

Willie smashed him on the back of the head with a hunk of lumber, knocking him head first into the trunk. Willie and I then pressed him, pulled him, punched him and stuffed him until finally we could close the lid. Willie snapped the hasp and stuck a hunk of wood through the loop to fasten it.

'That should hold him,' I said.

'Shall we call Scotland Yard?' asked Willie.

I thought a moment. The Russians evidently were after me, and now the Germans also. Scotland Yard would ask questions of Willie, and they might try telephoning Paris to intercept me. Scotland Yard might complicate things further. 'Leave him where he is, Willie,' I said. 'Let him ride back to London alone and boxed. Someone will find him eventually.'

'Won't they be surprised!' laughed Willie.

As we swayed and jiggled towards Dover we became aware of distant rumbling, then rain rushed on the roof, then Willie leapt to close the window.

'Coming down in sheets, Mr Holmes,' he said, wiping the rain off his face. ''Twill be a rough passage. I have some friends in Dover where you could stay, if you'd like to wait for the smoother water tomorrow.'

'Got to go over today, Willie.'

Willie grinned. 'You were always most fierce, Mr Holmes. Sometimes I wonder what you are made of.'

'This one is for king and country, Willie.'

'Then, I'm glad it is you, Mr Holmes. If anyone can carry it off, you can – whatever it is.' He grasped my shoulder with his big hand.

The carriage jolted to a stop along the platform at Dover

and we stepped out into a lashing rainstorm. The winds backed us up. We bent against the gale and made our way towards the steamboat. Willie insisted on carrying my valise, inside of which I hoped my disguises, clothes, revolver, and precious cargo were not getting wet. We waited in the transit building for an hour. At last we went down to the ship.

At the foot of the gangplank the purser stood checking tickets. Near him lingered an old woman who evidently was uncertain whether she dared make the crossing. She kept shaking her head. The white dog in her basket was whining.

'I would wait until tomorrow, madam,' said the purser. 'The sea will be much quieter.'

I handed him my ticket.

'Are you are up to it, sir?' said he, with a bluff smile. 'No guarantees!' He laughed heartily.

'I'll chance it,' said I.

I took the valise and shook Willie's hand. He hugged me. Then I started up the gangplank.

The dog in the old woman's basket began barking. Her shawl was soaked and her hair hung like a mop in front of her face, and her travelling bag was slouched at her feet. She struggled to gather it. 'I best go,' she said.

I paused, intending to help her with her luggage. But she stood so long in that wicked rain, fumbling so futilely to find her ticket, that finally I gave up on her and hurried up into the cabin.

The crossing was even rougher than promised, everything sliding, water boiling over the decks. When we neared Calais a sudden calm prevailed and ushered us in to port. I hurried away into the gloomy wet streets and found a small hotel and stayed the night, and in the morning I took the first train to Paris. On that dull October morning, as we clattered and whistled and steam-puffed through the bleak countryside, we could hear the roaring of the guns to the north where the Germans were driving south towards Ypres. I knew our British boys were in the thick of it, and that every bomb that exploded might well mean another five or ten English families would soon receive a telegram they would never forget. Our train often pulled into sidings and stopped while troop trains lumbered past. The troop trains were filled to overflowing with French lads. The lads looked gay and vigorous in their uniforms. They waved towards our train, where handkerchiefs in feminine hands fluttered like flowers from every window. After months in the trenches those hopeful and vigorous lads would look far from gay. But I think they didn't know it, for they were young. Thank god they didn't know it. And so we made our way towards Paris, amid the rumblings of war. By now the battle front stretched from the Channel all the way across the north of France to Switzerland. My urgent task was to find a route around that line of fighting, a route that would lead me into Germany and up to Berlin. My immediate plan was to travel through Paris and on to Geneva, thence to Bern and Basel, and so make my way north across the German border.

When I descended at the Gare du Nord I was shocked to realize that Paris, like the rest of the world, had changed. How strange to see motor vehicles crowding the boulevards! Who would have thought it? It seemed to me that everything in the world was changing, and that soon nothing would be the same. I took a motor taxi south across the river to the Rue des Beaux-Arts. That was the street where I had stayed during my previous visit to Paris, fifteen years earlier, in May of 1899. I tried to find the hotel where I had stayed in those early days, but it no longer existed. I walked twice past the section of street where it had stood. I thought memory had betrayed me. But the hotel was gone. I continued down the street and booked a room at the Hôtel d'Alsace. The name seemed vaguely familiar. I asked the desk clerk if this was where Oscar Wilde had died. It was.

I was interested in Oscar Wilde because I have always regarded theatrical performance as a required field of study for anyone serious about becoming a detective. As a student at Cambridge I spent many a pleasant and instructive hour acting in amateur theatrical productions – I may be the only Cambridge undergraduate who enrolled at the university in disguise, took rooms under an assumed name, and played a fictional role for several months before being unmasked by a fellow student. To escape from oneself into another character is the art of becoming invisible – an art I have practised throughout my career. I would have been dead many years ago had I not been a master of it. So naturally I followed the doings of the theatre world with great enthusiasm, and when Oscar Wilde's talent burst into view on the London stage in 1892, with 'Lady Windermere's Fan,' I was in the very first audience. After seeing that play I never missed the chance to attend a new Wilde production. But how quickly the golden days vanish for us all! Three years later, in 1895, 'The Importance of Being Earnest' appeared to overwhelming acclaim. And very swiftly thereafter came Wilde's fall from grace, and he was clapped in Reading Gaol. I remembered reading that he was released from prison, but after that I heard little of him. I had no notion of what had become of him until one day in Paris, in that spring of 1899, I encountered him quite unexpectedly by the Seine.

I was in Paris to help the Préfecture de Police with the Countess Pernod case, and I was turning the gruesome details of that astounding debauchery over and over in my mind as I descended the Rue Napoleon towards the river. I turned into the Quai D'Orsay and noticed an elegant woman strolling gaily along the quai just a few yards away. It was the opera singer Nellie Melba. I recognized her immediately, for I had seen her picture often in the magazines and newspapers which I daily ransacked for information that might be useful to my work. Madame Melba hummed cheerfully as she minced along, her chin high. Suddenly a tall, shabbily dressed man lurched out from around a corner. He accosted her. His collar was up. He looked like a highwayman. He said, 'Madame Melba, you don't know who I am? I'm Oscar Wilde. And I'm going to do a terrible thing . . .'

'Oh?'

'I'm going to ask you for money.'

Suddenly she seemed to recognize him. 'Oh, my!' she gasped. The shocked woman hastily began digging into her purse. She gave him several handfuls of money. Wilde bowed slightly, muttered, 'Thank you, my good Queen of Song,' and he quickly turned from her. Madame Melba gazed after him as he limped away. Then she hurried off along the quai, looking down and no longer humming.

That was a sad scene. And now, in 1914, looking back on those earlier days, I felt again how brief are life's bright hours. It seemed to me that, on the whole, those earlier days were happy ones, and that now the happy times were vanishing and ahead lay nothing but gloom. Every day in the newspapers were stories of war, disaster, death and uncertainty.

It was evening, dusk filling the streets as I checked into the Hôtel d'Alsace. I was given a ground floor room. I was quite certain I had not been followed to Paris but to be absolutely certain of anything is always dangerous. I pondered. In the days when Professor Moriarty and his men had pursued me through Europe I had often, after checking into one hotel, sneaked out in the night to another. But on this first evening in Paris, in 1914, I was so terribly weary that I decided to stay put. I would sleep. I would awake refreshed, gather what information I could about troop movements and new battle lines, and then I would plan the next phase of my journey to meet the Kaiser. Having made this decision, I went to bed and slept the sleep of the dead.

In the morning I walked out of the hotel feeling as energetic as Paris always made me feel. I strolled to the river and breakfasted on croissants and café noir. The air was sharp, the sun hazy. The barges tied up along the river looked leaden. As I strolled I calculated how long it would take me to get to the German border by travelling through Switzerland. When I reached the Place St Michel I saw a double line of French troops streaming toward me from the direction of Notre Dame Cathedral. Behind them the cathedral rose majestically. The soldier boys came across the bridge and into the Place and there they formed a great milling crowd. I silently wished them well. Then I walked up the angling little Rue St André des Beaux-Arts. When

I reached the Carrefour Buci I took a chair in a café and had another café noir. As I sat, gazing absently, I became aware of a young woman with a white toy poodle on a leash. She passed in front of me once, then passed again on the far side of the little square. But something was false about her. She seemed to be an actress playing a part, not a Parisian strolling a dog. In a flash I remembered similar scenes in the recent past. I thought of the woman walking the poodle outside Claridges, and the woman with the poodle walking in front of Willie Wiggins's apartment, and I remembered the sound of a small dog barking repeatedly during my trunk ride to the Charing Cross Station. I also remembered the old woman at Dover who had lingered and lingered at the foot of the gangplank until she learnt that I was going aboard, and how her face was muffled in a shawl, and how she held a small white dog in a basket. Now suddenly, in a Paris café, I realized that all those were the same person in different costumes. And the lost glove, yes! Evidently someone in Buckingham Palace had stolen it and given it to my pursuers, who had used it to give my scent to their tracking dog.

I sat in dull Paris sunshine, in weather almost too chilly to be comfortable, and watched an actress with a dog, and I wondered if maybe I was getting too old. My mental powers seemed to be fleeing, like the leaves of autumn. I sipped the last of my coffee and laid down my newspaper. I stood up briskly and strode out of the café into the Rue de Buci. I strolled, then darted into a side street and made my way back to my hotel in the Rue des Beaux-Arts. I walked with a soft step along the shabby hallway till I reached my room. I leant to touch the doorknob . . . but abruptly the doorknob was jerked out of my fingers and the door flew violently open. A tall young man stood before me. He waggled my own Webley revolver at me.

'Come in, Mr Holmes,' said he.

'Since you put it that way . . .' I said.

His thick black hair curled over his ears. When he smiled, the elegant scar on his cheek moved. I recognized him – he was the young man from Heidelberg, who had evidently won his badge of honour in a duelling society. 'You are no longer a chauffeur?' said I.

'That vas a temporary job, Mr Holmes. Chust sit down on that bed.'

I sat beside my open valise. He closed the door and waggled the end of the revolver. 'A little further away, a little further away from me, please.'

I moved back on the bed.

On the floor at his end of the room were the two camel-coloured leather cases. 'Two?' said he, waving a hand at them? 'Vee vere aware only of one.'

He spoke with a noticeable German accent, but his English was very good.

'They contain documents from King George meant only for the eyes of Kaiser Wilhelm,' I said.

'Ah, yes, vell, but some of us German subjects do not vish the conflict to end, now that it has begun. Vee vish Germany to vin, as indeed she vill. And that is why vee think it best to prevent the Kaiser from becoming, shall vee say, confused.'

'You have me at a disadvantage,' I said. 'I am in no position to argue with you.'

'You know, Mr Holmes, vee Germans respect genius. Vee do not vish to harm you. Vee vill relieve you of any documents that may trouble the Kaiser's peace of mind – then you may go your way.'

He lifted one of the small cases and laid it on the table. He clicked open the first latch, then the second. I was surprised he could do this. I had assumed both cases were locked. Then he lifted the lid and looked in. 'Was ist denn das!' he cried.

A moment later fire flashed upward and tore his head away. I was flung backwards hard against the headboard by the force of the explosion. My ears rang with pain. My nostrils were filled with mingled smells of burnt flesh and gunpowder. I stumbled to my feet. The headless corpse was smouldering on the carpet and the window behind it was blown out. I grabbed the other document case and packed it in the valise. I strapped my valise closed, rushed into the hallway. Already footsteps were thudding and shouts echoing. I ran into the street and turned the corner into the Rue Napoleon and kept running. When I reached the Quai D'Orsay I was exhausted. I hailed a taxi and it carried me to the Gare de Lyon. Undoubtedly the other conspirators had been watching the hotel, yet I had no evidence they had followed me. I hoped I had made my escape without detection.

At the Gare de Lyon I was fortunate. A train for Geneva was leaving in half an hour. I bought a ticket and hurried aboard a compartment in the middle of the train, taking the seat farthest from the window. A middle-aged woman and her husband entered the compartment and sat in the two window seats, facing each other. The woman stood up, lowered her window, and leant on it with folded arms as she hung her head out and gazed down the platform with a proprietorial air. I held my watch in hand, waiting impatiently as the hands jerked towards the moment of departure. The woman sat down and tidied herself. At last the train began to roll. We were on our way . . .

But now a man with a huge bald head floated into view, running hard down the platform. His handlebar moustache looked huge and his eyes glared and his cheeks were puffed out like balloons. It was the man Willie had knocked out in the baggage van at Canterbury. Here he was, again trying to board my train. His elbows were going like pistons, and every few strides he tried to grab the door handle. A slim dark man ran to the left of him, dropping behind as the train picked up speed. Once more the bald giant lunged for the door handle, missed, stumbled, and to save himself he grabbed the top of our open window with both his hands. He clung, he was dragged. The slim man shouted, 'Ludwig, du Dummkopf!' and vanished.

The platform flickered, disappeared.

Ludwig dangled in air, huge face pressed to our window pane.

The woman by the window humped to her feet and fled gasping out of the compartment. Her husband followed her.

I pulled off my boot and slammed Ludwig's knuckles

with its heel, pounded his fat knuckles until they began to seep blood. At last he howled and fell, and hit the gravel of the roadbed . . .

Ye gods, Wilson!

SIX

The World Interrupts

'A cat!' I cried, leaping to my feet. 'Just a cat.' But it had startled me, that scream! It sounded at first like a cry of the damned. A thrill of terror faded along my spine.

I had been listening so intently to my companion's narrative that only when the cat screamed did I become aware that Sergeant Bundle was knocking on our window. I opened the door.

'Good morning, gentlemen,' said Bundle. 'I stepped on the cat's tail. Poor fellow was sleeping.' Bundle's face was piled with smiles as he hunkered into the room and sat down in the chair I offered. 'Mr Coombes,' said he, 'you have put me on track!'

'Excellent!' cried Coombes, leaping from his chair and grabbing a spoon from the coffee table. He leant against the mantle and said, 'Pray give me the details.' He put the spoon into his mouth as if it were a pipe, and he waited with a languorous look in his eyes. 'Take your time and omit nothing,' he added.

Coombes's whole performance was so dramatic, and so odd, that it struck me as affected and phoney. Yet it certainly had the intended effect of settling the sergeant down to take his details very seriously. 'I have made an investigation into the question of what bicycles have been sold in the area in the past week. We have checked shops from here to Hereford and Brecon. A number of bicycles have been sold, but only two with tire treads that match the tracks in your photograph, Mr Coombes. One of those two was sold in Hereford to a young lad named Charles Montgomery. His father, also named Charles Montgomery, used a Visa card to pay for the bicycle. The bicycle is presently stored in their garage in Hereford. The other bicycle was sold in the same shop, on Widmarsh Street. I examined the man who sold the bicycle in some detail, Mr Coombes. He said the purchaser had thick sandy hair and bushy eyebrows, and he was dressed in blue jeans, a white shirt, a green suede jacket. He seemed to be about fifty but the sales clerk was strangely uncertain about this, and said he might have been younger. This customer bought the bike, paid cash, gave no indication of where he was from or where he was going. The salesman thought the customer was English and very upper class. No foreign accent at all.'

'Excellent work, sergeant,' said Coombes. 'And what of the victim's computer?'

'You were right again. The victim received a number of emails from someone who said she was Lydia Languish and who claimed to live here in Hay-on-Wye. We have not gone through all the emails yet, for there are hundreds, if not thousands. But it appears that the girl lured him here, just as you suggested. Unfortunately, we have not been able to connect the email address of Lydia Languish with the name of a real person. Our experts say that we may never accomplish this, although they are still working on the problem.'

'You will never find her,' came the reply, 'for Lydia Languish is a character in a play by Sheridan, called *The Rivals*, first performed in 1775.'

'Is she now?' said Bundle, nodding wisely. He shrugged with his big face. 'Also, sir, I found out the meaning of the Pashto words that were impressed into the dust jacket of the book. I passed them on to our mutual contact at Scotland Yard – you know who I mean—'

'Yes, yes of course . . .'

'And with the many resources of Scotland Yard, he called me back within the hour with the translation. The words mean, "God is great but we must do our own work".'

'We might postulate,' said Coombes, 'that our suspect is an actor fluent in English and also in Pashto.'

'That ought to narrow the field,' suggested Bundle.

'Perhaps,' said Coombes. 'But there are a great many

people in Britain who to some degree or other fit that description. They may be professional actors, amateur actors . . .' He shrugged. 'What else have you discovered, sergeant? I can tell by your manner that you are saving the worst news till last.'

'Well, sir, I'm afraid your theory is refuted. You imagined that revenge might be a motive for this crime, am I right?' said Bundle. 'And this was suggested to you by the book about Abu Ghraib.'

'The thought had crossed my mind,' said my friend.

'The trouble is, sir,' said Bundle, 'Mr Hawes served in Afghanistan only. He never was anywhere near Abu Ghraib prison in Iraq.'

I could see that this information disappointed Coombes. He nodded slowly, frowning slightly. Silence fell over both men. They were statues.

To fill the void I volunteered, 'What of Mr Jenkins? Has he been seen recently?'

'A very good point,' said Bundle. 'We cannot be perfectly sure that Mr Jenkins was in Scotland as he said he was.'

'Naturally,' I said, 'if he lured the American and murdered him, he would want to make it seem he was elsewhere.'

'But if it was Jenkins, how do we explain the book and the phrase in Pashto?' asked Bundle. He looked first at Coombes, then at me.

Coombes said nothing.

'Perhaps the book was only a prop,' I suggested. 'A deception. Elaborate, yes. But plays are elaborate. You said he was a theatrical manager.'

Bundle and I looked at each other hopefully. Coombes seemed uninterested.

'And one thing more,' said Bundle, 'the *Heigh-ho* on the mirror. I hardly know what to make of it . . . do you, Mr Coombes?'

Coombes suddenly snapped out of his reverie. He blinked, looked at Bundle. 'It, yes . . . it comes from the play. Lydia Languish says it repeatedly. You may recall, Bundle, that thirty years ago there was a very famous murder case in which the German word *Rache* was scrawled on a wall, in blood, by someone who hoped to throw investigators off the track . . . I'm sorry, not thirty . . . no, you wouldn't . . .' – he passed his hand over his forehead – '. . . more like a hundred and . . .' He frowned, seemed to drift away into another of his moods. Then he said, 'A meaningless phrase meant to confuse us.'

Sergeant Bundle took little notice. 'It sounds like mockery to me, sir – a phrase meant to mock the police.' He slapped his hand on the chair arm and got up.

Again Coombes was floating into some other realm, staring at the ceiling and drifting into outer space.

Bundle said his goodbyes and departed.

Suddenly the atmosphere in the room had become oppressive. I left my companion to his ruminations and walked to the top of the road and bought a newspaper. When I returned I saw that my moody companion had brought out his antique leather valise, the one with the *Hotel Beau-Rivage* sticker on the side, a valise of the sort people carried on board steamships in the days of the Titanic and Lusitania. It might have been on display at the Victoria and Albert. 'So this is your suitcase, is it?' I said. 'Your suitcase from 1914?'

'Exactly so,' he said. 'And it contains a positive treasure for dismal times like these.' He opened the valise and brought out a small morocco case a bit bigger than an eyeglass case. He opened the little case and withdrew a syringe. He gave a sigh as he sat down in his usual chair and rolled up his sleeve. I thought he might be ill, a diabetic perhaps. He seemed about to inject himself. I asked, as nonchalantly as I could, 'What are you doing?'

'The case has gone stale, Wilson,' he said. 'It is evident that more information is needed before it can be solved. And I have learnt by long and often bitter experience that the needed information may never arrive. A telegram, a telephone call, an unexpected visitor may come at any instant and set me back on a track that I can follow. Meanwhile, I am powerless. I warned you that these moods come upon me at certain periods. Inactivity is death to me. If I have practical problems to tackle, theories to concoct, puzzles to untangle, I can be happy. At those times my mind soars like a hawk, seeking the smallest bit of motion to dive upon and feed my insatiable curiosity in hopes of solving the problem. But when information has been utterly exhausted, when the trail has gone stale, when I have no challenge, no mystery, no paradox, no danger, no dilemma, not even any physical adventure, my brain and all the earth become a desert of boredom and commonplace, and then my oasis – which I need in order to survive – is a seven per cent solution of cocaine.'

'Come now, come now!' I said. I laughed heartily, albeit a bit tentatively. 'I can't believe what you are saying.'

'Old habits die hard,' he said.

'If it is really cocaine in your syringe,' I said, feigning indifference, 'I suppose you should know that nowadays using cocaine is illegal.'

'Quite legal for me, though,' he said. 'I have a special dispensation from Scotland Yard.'

'Hah!' I cried. 'That is difficult to believe, my friend.'

'It is perfectly true, my dear Wilson. My cocaine supply was prescribed by a doctor and certified by legal hocus-pocus at the highest levels of Scotland Yard. And now, if you'll excuse me, I am off to a lovely oasis, for it beckons me so enticingly that . . .'

I touched his shoulder. 'I hate to sound like a child, my friend, but please consider a moment – you have promised me a story. You have teased me by telling only half the story. That is not kind. That is not – if I may say so – honourable.'

He paused, staring at the tip of the needle as a lover stares trembling at the one he desires. I could see how much he craved it, how his promise was struggling with his private desire.

I urged him gently. 'Why not give both of us a little pleasure, you and me, by telling the rest of the story? You will enjoy it, I will enjoy it. A vicarious adventure for both of us. While you talk we'll have lunch at the Old Black Lion. I'll buy. Afterwards you can finish your tale as we take a walk up the long path to Hay Bluff. How does that sound, my friend! Lunch, climbing a bluff, and a tale of your adventures during The Great War – surely that should be nearly as good as a shot of cocaine!'

Slowly he set down the needle. He rolled down his sleeve. 'You should have been a diplomat,' he said. His grey-blue eyes were scintillant, lips pressed in half a smile. 'So you believe my strange tale, Wilson?'

'Whether I believe it I must yet discover. But you have told it in a most convincing manner. That cannot be denied. The suitcase –' I nodded towards it. 'Is it of 1914 vintage?'

'Much older than that, Wilson. I bought it in the '80s or '90s, and it became a good friend in my travels. It is a miracle that this old friend of mine made it through with me to the twenty-first century. By sheer good fortune my hand was gripping it in my last moments of 1914, and I was still clutching it when they found me in 2004. As a result, they had to cut the block of ice in which I was encased so that the block contained not only me but my valise. This slowed them down and made it difficult to transport me to London before I melted. So they told me.'

I laughed out loud. 'You'll have to forgive me, my friend,' I said. 'My laughter doesn't mean disbelief . . . not exactly, anyhow.'

'Shall we go?' asked Coombes. 'Let us fortify ourselves at the Black Lion, then head up to Hay Bluff.'

We closed the door of Cambrai Cottage and walked towards the Black Lion. As the clock tower in the village centre struck *one*, Cedric Coombes resumed his tale.

SEVEN
Pursuit

As I say, Dummkopf Ludwig was clinging to the window of my train compartment as we left Paris. He soon dropped away, however, and my two travel companions returned. The woman was very tidy. She wiped the blood off the window and closed the window tight. Thereafter we enjoyed a most pleasant train ride through French countryside, punctuated only by the distant thunder of an October storm. Thunder made the madame mistakenly fear she was hearing the German five-nines at the battle front. Her bespectacled husband and I both assured her that even the biggest of the German guns were too far away to be heard, and that she was hearing only God's cannons.

Say what you will about the Swiss, they know how to manage a country. Everything seemed just a little cleaner, quicker and less confused after we crossed the border and rolled into Geneva. I was waved through the frontier very quickly and soon had no more to do than find a comfortable hotel. From the train station I walked down the Rue du Mont Blanc to the lake, and there I turned left on to the Quai du Mont Blanc. I was soon attracted by the Hôtel Beau-Rivage where, for five francs a night, I booked a room with a view of the lake and the Alps beyond. The view alone was worth the price. The hotel had a French chef, and my supper was very fine. I ate slowly. I have never spent great effort developing a taste for food but I confess French food is my weakness, and although my nose is better trained for distinguishing the seventeen distinct types of tobacco smoked in Europe than it is for judging a wine's bouquet, yet I have always enjoyed wine and I indulged myself in a glass of fine wine that evening. As I ate and drank, I gazed out over the lake and considered my precarious situation.

King George had not kept his secrets very well. That was clear. Someone in his retinue had sneezed up the secret of my journey. The Germans knew my mission and they were following me. The Russians also knew, and they had tried to switch cases on me in order to assassinate the Kaiser with a bomb. But their bomb had blown up the wrong German, and the result was that the Germans, having no knowledge of the Russian plot, would now assume that I had killed their man, and doubtless they would now intend not merely to rob me but to kill me.

And then there was the problem of how to enter Germany. The border of Switzerland and Germany offered many routes of crossing. I was inclined to travel to the Bodensee, purchase a small sailboat at Romanshorn and sail across in the night to a landing spot somewhere near Friedrichshafen. From there I might travel north to Nuremberg, Leipzig, and Berlin – that is, if the Kaiser was still at Berlin. Recently (or so the newspapers informed me) he had been visiting his army in Belgium. Problem number one was to get into Germany. Problem number two was to locate the Kaiser – but that I could worry about later.

I folded my map, ate my dessert, drank my coffee, and occasionally gazed out over the blue lake at the strange white mountains rising to the south. Mont Blanc, the highest mountain in Europe, looked oddly small behind all the nearer peaks. In the dying light of evening I paged through my faithful *Baedeker's Switzerland,* 1913 edition. It informed me that the two-and-a-half hour steamer journey to Lausanne was far preferable to the railway journey. I took *Baedeker's* advice – one seldom goes wrong taking *Baedeker's* advice. Next morning I boarded the steamer.

The day was dull, the lake choppy and grey. Occasionally a flash of sun appeared through the clouds, turning the lake blue and the little shore towns white. I stood by the rail on the upper deck. Except for me, the deck was utterly empty, not a passenger to be seen. It was late October, windy, cold. I watched the town of Rolle drift by on the north shore.

Then I saw another passenger appear on the deck, a woman. She was pressing against the wind, leaning forward as she came towards me. What struck me as odd was her hat. It was a large Parisian flower hat, very pretty but not at all suitable for travel by steamer. Her little black dog strained ahead of her on his leash. I gazed at her curiously. It seemed clear that at any moment her beautiful hat would blow away. I wondered why she would wear such a hat on deck. Even as this question posed itself to my mind I noticed her shoes. They were not shoes suitable for a woman, and they did not go with her outfit. A pulse of alarm surged through my veins – too late. She looked up at me and smiled – and I saw she was not a woman at all. The knife was in his hand. He lunged at me.

At Cambridge I was considered a rather good amateur boxer. People said I had excellent strategy and surprising speed. I am happy to report that my Cambridge boxing experience served me well on the windy deck of the Lausanne steamship. I darted to the right, swung at his head, and landed a right hook that sent him tumbling over the rail. He fell as silently as a stone and plunged into surging waves that swallowed him. Someone hollered, 'Man overboard!' The Parisian hat, meanwhile, sailed away on the wind and settled on the wake far astern, where it bobbed like a little island of flowers.

The poor black poodle, having noticed his human friend fall into the lake, began to run up and down the deck, dragging his leash and barking frantically. Then he launched himself over the rail, tumbled head over tail, and vanished in the grey swells. He quickly reappeared, paddling desperately.

The massive steamship horn now resounded so suddenly and so close by that my whole body resonated. Steam rushed upward in grey clouds. The deck rocked. The steamer began to circle back. Somebody kept shouting 'Man overboard!' Suddenly a redheaded man darted on to the rear lower deck with both arms outstretched as if he were a tightrope walker. With a howl he stripped off his shirt. He dove over the side and landed with a shallow splash. He began furiously clawing the water of Lake Geneva. He headed straight towards the dog. He grabbed the poodle with one hand, then swam back towards the steamer in a lurching sidestroke, holding the dog out of the water. He reached the side of the ship and, surging upward, he miraculously grabbed hold of the rail. He swarmed over the side like an orangutan. His red hair streamed down his cheeks. Only then did I notice that the dog was suddenly white. White again. The dye had washed off.

I watched from the deck above as a crew member threw a blanket over the man's shuddering shoulders. The man cried, 'Danke, das ist schön!' and he walked away under the guiding arm of the solicitous crew member. From his affection for the dog, and his willingness to risk his life for it, I deduced that he must be the dog's owner and special friend.

I went to my cabin and sat down to count my enemies. The young German with the elegant Heidelberg saber cut on his cheek had been blown to pieces in my Paris hotel room. Dummkopf Ludwig had dropped on to a railway roadbed and was surely badly battered if not dead. The multiple transvestite actor – the London lady who walked her dog by Claridges, the mother who strolled her pooch in front of 221B Baker Street, the old crone who held her dog in a basket in the rain at Dover, and the Parisian charmer who crossed the Carrefour de Buci with her trotting poodle – had been drowned. Apparently so, anyhow. No one had spotted a body floating and already the steamer had stopped circling and had set its course for Lausanne. That left only the redheaded man. His physical prowess seemed prodigious. But what made him most dangerous was the dog. I knew that as long as that poodle was on the prowl he might come across my scent and track me down.

I opened my valise and pulled out false whiskers, false eyebrows, a beret, and a long coat. I transformed myself into Monsieur Vaucluse, a scholar from Bordeaux. Then I went down to the restaurant and ordered a meal, keeping a sharp lookout for the redheaded man known to me only as 'the orangutan'. When the steamer reached Ouchy, the port of Lausanne, I made sure I was the first passenger off on to the pier, and that I was not seen by either the orangutan or his dog. I struggled up the steep street with my valise and eventually found a hotel in the Rue de la Gare, close by the railroad track of the Swiss Federal Line. This rail line lies about three-quarters of a mile above the port of Ouchy and about a half mile below the town of Lausanne. I signed the register as Monsieur Vaucluse. In my room I changed my costume and became Mr T.J. Clapper, a very old gentleman from Finsbury Park, London. I left the hotel by the side door, carrying with me the King's attaché case and a cloth bundle of disguises. I hastened into a grove of pine trees nearby and hid myself. I watched as the surge of passengers from the steamer slowly rose up the street like the tide. Some passengers were on foot, some in vehicles. I spotted the redheaded man carrying a heavy trunk on his shoulder. Ahead of him his little white poodle zigzagged with its nose to the ground, sniffing furiously this way and that, sometimes losing my scent in his haste and then picking it up again almost immediately. He led his simian master straight to the front door of my hotel. The orangutan lowered his trunk and pulled out a handkerchief and mopped his brow, then tied the dog to the handle of the trunk and went inside the hotel. He emerged about five minutes later, having doubtless extracted from the innkeeper the name of the last guest who had checked in, a Mr Vaucluse from Bordeaux, room 202. The redheaded man untied the dog, hefted the trunk, but did not turn into the street. Instead he walked around the back of the building and looked at the upper stories. Evidently he was trying to locate room 202. He stood for a long while, gazing upward. Then he inspected the black iron drain pipe that ran up the side of the building. Finally he turned away and headed up the road towards Lausanne, swaying side to side with the rolling gait of a sailor. The little dog ran merrily beside him.

I emerged from the grove of pine trees and followed them at a distance, glad I was carrying no more than the King's small case. Lausanne is very steep town. That is why most people use the funicular that runs from the lake to the town centre. The man and dog entered a hotel. When I was sure they intended to remain there, I turned away and descended a few hundred yards in the direction of the lake, and then I wandered eastward until I espied a very pleasant hotel called the Britannia. There I registered under the name T.J. Clapper. My room was large and bright. I hid King George's leather case behind the huge armoire in the corner. After supper I changed back into my 'Monsieur Vaucluse' get-up and descended in the dark to my hotel in the Rue de la Gare. I did not enter, however. Instead, I stood in the grove of pine trees, growing colder and colder as I watched the back of the hotel. Overhead, the moon blew through clouds like a ship, travelling slowly across the sky. About eleven o'clock I perceived a dark figure emerge from the blotted shadows of the street. It slid along the white building. It stopped at the cast iron drainpipe. The creature gave a little leap and went up the pipe as quickly as a monkey. I was astonished how easily he reached the first floor. He popped open a window and vanished into room 202.

Eventually a dim electric light came on in my room. The orangutan's shadow flickered on walls and panes as he ransacked the place, evidently searching for the attaché case. After half an hour the electric bulb went off. He reappeared in the window. He looked fearsome, lit by the quarter light of the startling moon. In an instant he had slathered down the drain pipe and was hurrying away across the lawn like an ape, knuckles almost dragging on the road. I was very cold by then. I went up to my room and straightened the mess. I slept a few hours until dawn.

The following day I kept careful track of all train traffic along the main line, noting at what hours trains appeared, from what direction, and the interval of time that elapsed between the first moment I could hear a train and the moment it passed me. I also, in the guise of T. J. Clapper, hobbled around Lausanne and noted the habits of the orangutan and his poodle companion. I jotted in my notebook what hour they emerged from their hotel, where they stopped for refreshment, how long they spent criss-crossing the city trying to pick up my track. On many occasions I saw the redheaded man stoop and hold my glove in front of the dog's nose, urging him on. Many times the little creature really did pick up my scent, and then he would set off running merrily, full of joy, earnestly nosing this way and that while the orangutan, far behind him, hurried to catch up. It was a queer feeling, seeing myself followed while I followed the followers. Several times when I saw them coming my direction I took elaborate evasive measures so that the dog would not lock on to my fresh scent and corner me.

On the third day all my information was complete. I could guess when the orangutan and his poodle would be at the café outside their hotel, and I knew precisely how long it would take me to run from the café to the train crossing at the Avenue Juste Olivier. I am not a cruel man, Wilson. On many occasions in the streets of London I have beaten a cabman for beating his horse – one of the many aspects of my eccentric character that Dr Watson tactfully left out of his narratives. But you will remember that I was on a mission to save millions of soldiers and civilians from death and mayhem. To do so I needed to rid myself of this innocent little beast who had tracked me halfway across Europe.

At eight thirty precisely, the redhead sat down – as he had the previous day – at a small table outside his usual café. The perky poodle lay prettily beside him. I strolled by their table at eight thirty-two, dressed in my long coat as Monsieur Vaucluse. The dog sensed me. His head swung around and his ears popped up. He leapt to his feet and began barking. When I saw the dog coming after me, I began to run. I glanced back and saw the orangutan rising from his table, but by then I was far ahead. As I reached the railroad crossing I could hear the train approaching from the east, exactly on schedule. I ran westward, skipping right down the middle of the tracks, hopping along those sleepers like a rabbit, my coat flowing out behind me. I am pretty spry for a man of my age, truth to tell. I had it all timed, carefully calculated. In any country but Switzerland my plan might not have worked, but the Swiss run their trains to the second. I leapt off the tracks at the place I had previously marked. When I looked back I saw the little white poodle running with his nose an inch from the sleepers. He was so furiously fascinated by my scent that he was unaware of the train closing in on him from behind. The redheaded man, meanwhile, was hurrying along beside the tracks, trying to keep up with the dog. He shouted, but the poodle paid no heed. As the train hurtled closer, the orangutan leapt on to the tracks – wonderfully agile – and he leant, scooped up the dog, and for an instant I thought he had saved him . . . but then the orangutan stumbled, fell head first between the rails. An instant later the engine gobbled him up, smeared him along the right of way. I saw his severed leg lying by the side of the track, still gushing blood. The train passed and then I saw his severed right arm lying by itself on the far side of the track. His body was dragged a hundred feet further on. He lay face down on the sleepers. By some miracle the poodle had popped out of danger and had begun running back and forth alongside the tracks, back and forth just as he had done on the deck of the steamship, distraught and confused.

I hurried away to Monsieur Vaucluse's hotel and got my valise. Then I walked to Mr Clapper's hotel and pulled the attaché case from behind the armoire and packed it. I emerged from the hotel as Mr Sherlock Holmes, wearing my grey trousers, white cotton shirt, black silk tie, black frock coat, vest, plus my overcoat of wool and my bowler. I sallied forth a confident man.

The morning had started bright with sunshine but now, as I boarded the train for Freiburg, heavy clouds had begun forming over the lake and mountains. The train slid out of the Lausanne station at a crawl, passing slowly by men working near the tracks with stretchers and baskets, still busily cleaning up body parts. Rumour had flown through the town that someone had been killed on the tracks – a suicide it was said – and many passengers stood up and looked out the windows. Most regretted having done so. I saw several turn away with horrified faces and sit down looking sick, muttering and gasping. I opened my morning paper to read the latest war news. I learnt that the fighting still raged at Ypres, but that so far the British and French line was holding. Later the world would learn that in the battle for Ypres alone the Germans lost about 130,000 soldiers, the British 60,000, the French 60,000. As I travelled towards Frieburg and Bern that morning, no one knew the final count, but even then my newspaper reported enormous casualties. Such staggering numbers made me feel I must get to Cousin Willy as quickly as possible with the documents from Cousin Georgie. Every day, every hour, men were dying in their hundreds. The sooner I delivered the documents the sooner the carnage might cease. At the same time, I became more and more doubtful that this small packet in my care could stop such a holocaust.

At Freiburg the train stopped awhile, and I was again startled and stunned, for when I leaned out the train window I saw Dummkopf Ludwig hopping along the platform on one crutch. His shoulder was bandaged and he had scratches all over his face and head. I regretted not having grabbed my trusty Webley from the Heidelberg corpse in my Paris hotel room. I began to feel I was in a bad dream that would never end. It was Ludwig, all right. His huge bald dome of a head and his walrus moustache were unmistakable. At each train window he lurched upward to look in, and at each lurch his arms flapped a little, as if he were a giant bird. I sat down quickly and hid behind my newspaper. I felt he had not seen me. But I wasn't entirely sure. How could I be?

When the train arrived at Bern I jumped out of my carriage and hurried to the train board almost at a dead run. There I discovered that an express was leaving shortly for Interlaken, another for Basel. I ran for the Basel train but missed it. I then ran for the Interlaken train and barely managed to heft my valise aboard as the carriages started to roll. Again, I could not be sure that Ludwig had not seen me board that train. So although it was late in the afternoon when I arrived in Interlaken, and although I was very tired and very tempted to find a hotel and call it a day – and spend a pleasurable evening consulting *Baedeker* about possible routes into Germany . . . yet I dared not. I waited in a dark corner of the station until the next train from Bern arrived. As I had feared, Ludwig bounded off even before the carriages had come to a stop. He flailed his way through the station, occasionally whacking people with his elbows. He hurried to a newspaper kiosk. There he lingered. He craned his neck and hopped in an agitated manner. Obviously he was looking for someone. Finally he gave up and hurried out into the street. He looked anxiously this way and that, up and down the avenue. All his actions suggested to me that he must have telegraphed ahead from Bern, contacted someone, told them to watch for me and follow me to my hotel. Evidently the spy was then to meet him by the kiosk to inform him of my whereabouts. The fact that no one had yet met Ludwig meant that whoever was watching me was *still* watching – baffled because he could not meet Ludwig without me observing them meeting. I decided to bide my time. Outside the station wall I set down my valise and opened a newspaper and hid behind it. I waited until Ludwig hurried back inside the station. Then I waited a few moments longer, to allow his contact to decide it was safe to leave me for a moment to dart inside and meet Ludwig. Quickly I stepped into the street, waved for a motor-taxi. A moment later I was on my way to the west train station.

At the Ost station I boarded the Oberland Railway train to Lauterbrunnen. A pleasant journey of three-quarters of an hour brought me to that little village. I descended to the platform feeling exhausted but relieved. As I walked away from the train, a young woman with a white toy poodle came towards me. I felt a pang of uncertainty. But the dog paid no attention to me. Neither did the woman. I walked to the pleasant Hotel Staubbach, about eight minutes from the train station, and there I booked a room. Like any sensible fox who has been hunted to exhaustion, I decided to go to ground and not move, and let the pack wear itself out. I hoped the German schweinhunds would give up and go home.

Lauterbrunnen is a pretty, scattered village lying on both

banks of the Lütschine, situated in a rocky valley about a
half mile wide. Into that valley (as my *Baedeker* warned)
the sun's rays do not penetrate before seven a.m. in July
or before eleven a.m. in winter. In one direction, rising
above the huge rocky precipices of the Schwarze Mönch,
are the snowy heights of the Jungfrau. In the other direction soars the Breithorn.

Near my hotel were the well-known Staubbach Falls –
the name means 'spray brook.' After breakfast the first
morning I took a five-minute walk and gazed up at this
famous falls. Almost a thousand feet above me a meagre
stream leapt from a jutting rock. Most of the stream was
converted into spray as it fell, and in the morning sun it
resembled a silvery veil wafted to and fro by the breeze. I
strolled through the rock gallery beneath the falls. A little
farther down the path I came upon a prim little man kneeling
on the ground beside a walking stick and a case of test
tubes. He was very neatly dressed in a brown suit and brown
hat. He was collecting samples of water from a spring. He
corked the tube in his hand, wrote a number on the label
with his pencil, and as he put the labelled specimen into
the case he looked up and noticed me. He quickly got to
his feet and, giving a little bow, he said, 'Ah, Mr Sherlock
Holmes, I presume? How very surprising to meet you here
in Switzerland in time of war. I am Professor Zimmerman.'

I was startled to find my identity so easily discovered. I
greeted the professor with reserve.

The professor's pristine white shirt had been freshly soiled
with dirt, his fingers were stained by chemicals, his trouser
cuffs were wet. He swept his vest briskly with the backs
of his hands. 'I see you are surprised, Mr Holmes, that I
recognise you. You see, I never forget a face.'

'Neither do I,' said I. 'And that is why I know I have
never met you.'

'Ah, pardon me!' cried Zimmerman. 'Let me explain, sir:
I recognise you from a photograph published in a maga-
zine about twenty years ago. On that occasion you had just
sent the notorious Professor Moriarty to his death at a place
not far from here.'

'At Meringen,' I said.

'Yes, the Reichenbach falls,' he said. 'It was thought at the time that you had died with him. I remember the pictures of you two gentlemen, side by side.'

Professor Zimmerman picked up his stick and case of tubes, and we walked together back up along the path. Several times he stopped, uncorked a tube, filled it with a sample of water from a spring, corked the tube, labelled it, and put it into the case with the other tubes. I asked him the object of his sampling, but he was reluctant to answer. He said he kept his research secret since very few of his fellow citizens would approve of him if they knew what he was up to. Half, he said, would think him mad, and the other half would think him a heretic. I did not press him. I talked casually on other subjects as we strolled, for I sensed he was anxious to reveal his secret and would tell me in good time. As we neared the village he said that he viewed me differently than he viewed most people, since I was a scientific man. He asked if I would care to see his laboratory. I said I would, and he led me to a small cottage and showed me in. One room was dedicated entirely to his researches. It was filled with distilling apparatus, chemicals in bottles and cans, Bunsen burners, and so on. In a large cage were two alpine choughs, one of whom was, according to Professor Zimmerman, a hundred and ten years old. The other, he said, was a little younger. Their age was proved, he said, by metal tags which had been clipped to their legs in 1810 by a birdcatcher named Dolman. Dolman's Choughs, he told me, had drunk the waters of Lauterbrunnen since they were chicks. This, he believed, was the secret of their great age. His researches were dedicated to finding a Spring of Youth, or, as he preferred to call it, an Eternal Elixir made from a mixture of spring waters whose beneficial minerals he was attempting, first, to isolate, and then to enhance by addition of certain other minerals and chemicals.

I was now anxious to get back to my hotel but Professor Zimmerman would not let me go easily. He enthusiastically led me to his kitchen and urged that I try a flask of his concoction. He said he had been drinking it himself. He said he was astonished at the vitality it infused into him. He said that if I drank it and liked it – that is, if I felt better and healthier – I might consider testing a month's supply for him. He showed me a flask, all carefully labelled. It looked so fresh and inviting after our brisk walk that I agreed to try it. As you know, Wilson, I have always been willing to use my own body to test my own scientific theories, so I thought nothing of drinking Zimmerman's Eternal Elixir.

If I had not drunk it I would not be here speaking to you today. I am not sure whether I owe Zimmerman my thanks or my disgust, because as yet I have not decided whether living as long as I have lived is an advantage or a mistake. But in any case he is the one responsible for sending me into the twenty-first century.

EIGHT

The Elixir of Suspended Animation

'Come now, Coombes!' I laughed – I leant back in my chair in the cheerful warmth of the Old Black Lion Inn, and I set my beer on the table. 'You almost had me believing in your tale! But when you tell me it was thanks to having drunk Professor Zimmerman's Eternal Elixir that you are a hundred and fifty-four years old, I'm afraid you have gone beyond the bounds of my credulity.'

'What!' said my companion, looking startled.

'It's all good fun,' I said, 'and I'm as good a sport as any man, but I'm feeling a bit victimized, I can tell you. Obviously you have secrets that you are keeping from me, hiding them behind a veil of fantasies. So be a good fellow, Coombes, and tell me – what is this charade all about? Oh, and a bit of advice – the art of telling a tall tale is to know when to stop. All morning you've had me almost believing you were really Sherlock Holmes himself, returned from the dead. But now, my dear Coombes, you have spoilt it.'

Coombes looked abashed, as if I'd slapped him. He tilted his head slightly, raised his napkin, daintily dabbed his lips. 'I only meant – my dear Wilson – that Zimmerman made me deathly sick with his brew. This sickness set in motion a train of events that led to my eventual appearance here with you in the restaurant of the Old Black Lion Inn, where I am enjoying your company.'

'Ah, well that sounds more plausible,' I said.

But I wasn't really convinced.

We paid our tab and stepped out into the bright and blowy November streets of Hay.

'Still game for a stroll up the hill to Hay Bluff?' I asked.

'Absolutely,' said he.

We crept through a little passageway leading off the street, walked past barking dogs, and started up the track to Hay Bluff. The path soodled across a sheep pasture and dribbled upward into woods. We crossed a stile with an acorn painted on it. Soon the town vanished behind us. Up and up we walked over green swells, up over more stiles, up and up over a grassy knoll that soared above the roof of a house mostly hidden far below in trees.

'There it is,' he said, pointing. 'The Old Vicarage cottage. It must be from here that Jenkins's friends saw the lights on, which prompted them to call the police the following morning, and to ask Sergeant Bundle to investigate whether Jenkins had really returned from Scotland, or whether the house had been burgled.'

'Have you considered interviewing those two friends of Jenkins?'

'It would be useless, Wilson. We have come to a gloomy dead-end in this case. And that, please understand, is what drove me to reach for my cocaine. I thought I had escaped from that vicious habit many years ago! But the old desire resurfaced the moment I awoke in the twenty-first century. No sooner did I find myself lying in the utter boredom of a hospital bed at St Bart's, in close proximity to medicines of all varieties, than the thought of cocaine occurred to me. Before long the undisguised desire for it assailed me. Perhaps something in the process of reviving me caused a relapse.'

'Telling me the rest of your tale may divert your mind,' I said.

'Yes,' he said, breathlessly.

We had just reached the high end of a steep field of sheep.

'Let's halt for a moment,' I said.

'Excellent idea.'

We paused by a wall. We turned, and gazed down at the huge hilly landscape falling away below.

'So the real truth is that Professor Zimmerman's elixir proved faulty?' said I.

'In the Pantheon of Famous Quacks,' he replied,

'Zimmerman of Zurich is right up there with Mesmer of Paris, Jesus of Nazereth . . .'

'Holmes!' I cried. 'You call Jesus of Nazareth a Famous Quack! That must be the first time in history that he has been so characterized! I never imagined you to be a man who had contempt for the beliefs of others!'

'Contempt is not the right word, Wilson. But I must confess that my dear friend and biographer, Dr Watson, always suppressed my more outré thoughts. He feared alienating large portions of the reading public. I am sure you know how he felt, Wilson, for you have been a professional writer all your life. No doubt you would suppress much of my character if you wrote about me.'

'I don't think I would suppress anything,' I said indignantly. 'If readers do not like my truth, let them read something else. Their tastes are their own, but my taste is for truth – or, at least, as close to truth as I can manage. But tell me, whatever can you mean by the remark that Jesus is a quack?'

'I mean that Jesus did a lot of magical curing of madness, blindness and so on. His holy stunts were not exactly quackery, perhaps, but they gave rise to several millennia of charlatans. That is not a record that does him credit. Not to mention that by raising Lazarus from the dead he inspired a host of mad scientists to try schemes of the Victor Frankenstein variety.' Holmes laughed suddenly. 'Come to think, the Frankenstein trick may not have been so astounding as I once imagined.'

'You feel rested?' I asked.

'Quite.'

'Then let us head for *points up*, shall we?'

'Away, Wilson!' cried he, lifting his walking stick as if it were a long sword.

And so we continued our upward journey.

'Where did I leave off?' he asked.

'Professor Zimmerman.'

'Ah,' said Holmes. And then he resumed his tale.

'Zimmerman, yes. Professor Zimmerman stood there holding out the flask with his stained fingers, smiling expectantly. It was only because he was so enthusiastic about his concoction that I humoured him and took a swig or two. He then urged me to finish the entire flask, just to be certain I would realize its full effects by the end of the day. In for a penny, in for a pound, thinks I, and I quaffed it off. I thanked him for his hospitality, then walked briskly back to my hotel. But soon I began to feel queasy, dizzy, hot, achy. My stomach would not be quiet. Gas pains. By day's end I had experienced the full effects of Zimmerman's elixir, just as he had promised – only I had not expected those effects would be vomiting, diarrhoea, sweats, chills, headache, dizziness and high temperature. I tumbled into bed and stayed for a week. I was delirious, defecating, vomiting. By the end of the second week I was dehydrated, exhausted, and I had become thinner. I remember faces leaning over me as I lay in my bed. One was the fat red face of a doctor they had brought up from Interlaken. He gave me medicines and disappeared like a dream. I remember Zimmerman's face leaning over me too. He had come to see if I had experienced an increase in animal spirits after drinking his concoction, and he was surprised to find me almost dead. His prim little moustache twitched slightly as he tried to plumb the depth of my misery. He was sympathetic, but helpless. I knew it was his flask of Eternal Elixir that had done me down, for no one else at the hotel was ill. But I did not tell Zimmerman this.

'After two weeks the illness receded. I began to eat again. I ventured out. I rambled through the village on wobbly legs. Every day I felt stronger. I decided my pursuers must have long since given up and gone home to Germany. After three more days of rest I would pack my valise and start my journey to the German border.

'But the following morning clouds moved in, snow began to fall, fell steadily all day. Snow continued falling the next day, too. And the next. The Bernese Oberland Railway trains were still running, so we got the newspapers from Interlaken, and we read that blizzards had blown on to the battlefields of France and that our troops were freezing to death in the trenches. One morning I awoke and looked out and saw

strange tracks in new snow below my bedroom window. I
hurried outside to investigate. Streaks and gouges and cock-
eyed footsteps indicated that a man with a crutch had circled
the hotel, had stood in one spot a long while, and then had
headed back towards the village centre.

'Perhaps the doctor who had come up from Interlaken
to attend to me had also attended Ludwig's leg, and had
informed him of my whereabouts. Or perhaps I was discovered because of Zimmerman, who had recognized me
as Sherlock Holmes. He had told other people, with the result
that soon everyone in the hotel was calling me Mr Holmes.
Could it be that the rumour of a famous English detective
(pardon this suggestion, Wilson!) – I say, that the rumour
of a famous English detective residing in Lauterbrunnen
had spread down the mountain and out into the valleys, and
Ludwig had gotten wind of it?

'The time had come for me to leave. I purchased an old
pair of boots from the innkeeper. I put on a sweater and
overcoat, wrapped my head in a scarf, donned my gloves,
and set forth for the station, lugging my valise. I considered
going down the mountain to Interlaken via the Bernese
Oberland Railway, and thence on to Zurich. That would
have been the most sensible thing to do. But it would also
be exactly what Ludwig would expect me to do.
Alternatively, I could take the Wengern Alp Railway up the
mountain to Kleine Scheidegg, and from there I could switch
cars and go down to Grindelwald on the far side . . . or else
from Kleine Scheidegg I could do the seemingly ridiculous
and take the Jungfrau Railway up to a dead-end railway
station (the highest in Europe) atop the Jungfraujoch. As I
walked towards the Lauterbrunnen station the snow began
to fall in great blinding whirls. I nearly lost my way. When
I reached the station house I peered in through the fogged
window before entering. I saw Ludwig in a greatcoat
hunkered by the stove. His moustache and Russian fur hat
made him look like a Cossack. I remained outside in the
storm. By and by the train for Kleine Scheidegg arrived,
moving more slowly than usual, its light burning a hole in
the whirling snow. I hurried towards the track, climbed into

the first car, ducked down. A few other passengers boarded.
The train started up. I thought I might have made my escape.
Then I looked back and saw Ludwig sitting in the car behind,
smiling at me. He pulled out a large hunting knife and ran
his thumb along the blade, and smiled again. He seemed
in no hurry to finish his mission. Evidently, now that he
had me, he intended to enjoy the *coup-de-grace*. What
worried me was not that he had a knife but that he had
showed it to me. I wondered whether he was trying to lull
me into thinking that the knife was his only weapon, whereas
perhaps he also had a firearm.

'Suddenly snow stopped and sun burst through the clouds
and the world turned dazzling: the valley spread out below
us like a huge painting. We could see for many miles. Up
and up we travelled. When we reached the station at the
saddle of the mountain I stepped out of the train carriage
and walked quickly towards the train waiting to descend to
Grindelwald on the far side. Ludwig lurched towards the
same train, pressing his way through the other travellers. I
had no notion whether he intended to take my valise, my
life, or both. I jumped aboard a middle car and bent down
in my seat so as not to be seen. When the train was about
to leave I slipped out of the carriage and into the snow. The
train slid away.

'But then I saw Ludwig leap out and go sprawling on
the snow. I hurried uphill out of his view. The sensible thing
to do now, I thought, would be to board the train back to
Lauterbrunnen. But undoubtedly Ludwig would expect me
to do this. He would do the same, which would leave me
right back where I started. Therefore I hurried to the Jungfrau
Railway and boarded a car. This made no sense whatever
– which is why I thought I might get by with it. I would
ride to the top of the Jungfraujoch, look around, and decide
if I could stand staying out all night in the cold. If so, I
would remain up there when my train (which was the last
train of the day) descended. I would be safe for the night,
though I knew I would suffer from cold. In the morning I
would ride down and take a train to Grindelwald.

'So there I sat in the Jungfrau Railway car, hoping for

escape. But just before our scheduled departure, Ludwig came batting and hopping his way towards my train. He boarded it and sat in the back. In the middle of my car passengers from Grindelwald were laughing. The doors closed. We began to ascend over snowy pastures. We could see the Jungfrau and the mountains of the Lauterbrunnen Valley. After passing through a tunnel we reached the Eigergletscher station at seven or eight thousand feet. The restaurant appeared to be closed. My faithful *Baedeker* described this station as being situated amidst a 'scene of wild magnificence' at the foot of the west arête of the Eiger. Perfectly true. The train whirred and continued upward. I paged through my *Baedeker* and tried to develop a plan.

'Most railways ascend the outside of a mountain. The Jungfrau Railway is unusual in that it travels up the inside of the mountain. Soon we entered the main tunnel and angled upward steeply. At about 9400 feet we reached the Eigerwand station, one of the stations excavated from solid rock. Openings were cut in the rock so passengers could look right out of the mountain and enjoy stupendous views of Grindelwald, the lakes of Brienz and Thun, and a large part of Western Switzerland. We lurched away from Eigerwand and continued upward through the electrically lighted tunnel, straining and chugging another thousand feet till we reached Eismeer in the southeast face of the Eiger. This station, too, was excavated from solid rock. I noted its layout carefully. I had begun to form a desperate plan. The restaurant, I saw, was closed. Four of our group felt dizzy and wished to go no further, so they got out. We continued upward, ascending through the inside of the mountain until at 11,340 feet we came out on to the top, to the station on the Jungfraujoch. I walked to the terrace and mingled with the tourists from Grindelwald, all of whom were Swiss. The war had deterred foreign visitors. Ludwig hovered nearby and gazed into distance. Far away the world was at war, but here was peace. Dark was already settling upon the mountains. Overhead, stars had begun to appear in the purple. The cold was intense. The cold seemed to increase as we stood there.

'Ludwig made no move. I returned to the train car with the Swiss group. The train jerked and started down the mountain. A new plan was whirling in my head. All the information on which it was based came from my trusty *Baedeker*. We stopped at Eismeer station. The four people who had gotten out there now re-boarded the train. I waited, carefully waited until the electric motors began to whir. And then, just as the train began to glide, I jumped out on to the platform with my valise. I had escaped! Or so I thought. Then I heard a yowl and saw a crutch jam itself in the train door: Ludwig tumbled out on to the rocky roadbed and hit hard.

'The train disappeared downward and its sound faded.

'I darted away into the pedestrian tunnel that led out to the glacier. When I got to the bottom of it I slipped around the corner, out of view, and there I crouched under the night sky and waited. The electric lights of the station showed dimly far out on the snow. Slowly the sky faded black. My hope was that Ludwig was severely injured – mortally injured, preferably. I knew he had a crutch and a knife. I could not be certain what other weapons he carried. I bitterly regretted that when I had had him in that trunk at Canterbury I had not shipped him to Scotland Yard as Willie Wiggins had suggested. I would have saved myself a deal of trouble.

'I grew colder. The full moon rose. All the vast earth – the valleys, the mountain ranges, the lakes – made a moonlit scene more beautiful than ever I had witnessed.

'"Holmes!" he cried.

'The shout echoed down the cold tunnel.

'"Holmes!" he cried. "Wo bist du!"

'I peeked around the corner and saw his hulking shape silhouetted at the top of the tunnel; a bear leaning on a crutch.

'He hollered, "Holmes! I vant the case! I vill leave you your life."

'He could not know if I was armed. I thought he might retreat. He turned and walked towards the restaurant with a tentative and uncertain air, the air of a man who is puzzling over his next move.

'Quickly I got to my feet and walked out on to the snow of the glacier. I headed down.

'I knew from my *Baedeker* that the Bergli Hut was an hour and a half away. I could see its distant roof. *Baedeker* sternly recommended a guide for anyone who tried to reach the hut, warning of falling stones and dangerous ice. I had determined to try to reach the hut without a guide. I had no choice. If I made it I would certainly find shelter for the night, and maybe even food. If I was very lucky I might encounter a party of mountaineers descending. I had heard rumours of climbers who had been caught by the snows and were trying to get down. This, of course, was unlikely. Most probably I would need to find my own way down to the valley and to civilization in the morning. I had no idea whether this was even possible.

'For half an hour I picked my way down and down through the snow. All the deceptions of the mountains were doubly deceptive by moonlight. Many times I came to a drop-off that had been hidden until I reached it. Then I was forced to backtrack and try another route. It was on one of these occasions, as I was turning around to backtrack, that I saw Ludwig. His huge dark figure tilted and skittered and hopped across the brow of a snowy crest. He looked like something out of a comic opera. What a fantastic scene it was, Wilson! There was this huge, dark, bearlike figure flailing towards me. Behind him hung a stupendous backdrop of towering white peaks and millions of stars in blackness, and closer by were streams of snow blowing off ridges like white fire. Suddenly Ludwig's monstrous figure stumbled and with a cry he began to slide. I hoped he might slide into a crevasse so I could climb back up to Eismeer station. No such luck. He halted his slide by dragging his crutch in the snow. He got to his feet, much closer now. He dug into the pocket of his greatcoat. I saw the gleam of a pistol in moonlight. The drop-off was below me, Ludwig above. I fell to my stomach on the snow. I heard a bullet *zing*, then a *crack*. He fired the pistol twice more in rapid succession. The sounds echoed away and became a strange roar.

'The mountain behind him had begun to move.

'The roar grew louder. White slabs of mountainside dropped straight down, intact, like massive walls, and then disintegrated into a boiling flood of white, and the flood of white formed a massive wave, and the wave hit Ludwig and flipped him like a doll, and he rose high into the air and then fell back and was buried, sucked away, and I saw his crutch skittering and leaping and hopping by itself atop the surging flood.

'I rolled on to my back. I took a deep breath. I closed my eyes. Make best use of all your time – that is what my father always told me. I decided to practise my Zen meditation in my remaining few seconds. It was all I had time for. A wall of cold wind fluttered my clothes. A terribly cold wind hit me. Then my mother appeared and threw a blanket on to me. But the blanket was cold and pressed down upon me very heavily. I felt the ice seeping into my brain.

'A moment later I opened my eyes and looked for mother. But she was gone. I realized I was in St Bart's hospital, the new wing. I realized this because I recognized the ceiling moulding. I was in the very room, as it turned out, where I had once beaten corpses with sticks to ascertain how much a body might be bruised after death. I later learnt that this was now the old wing of the hospital. But that was later. At the moment I was merely puzzled as to why I was lying in bed instead of tending to my lab experiments.

'A nurse appeared. She flung her left hand to her lips. "Oh," she cried, "you're awake at last!"

'"I'm cold," I said. But I could barely say those two words. I had trouble speaking.

'She leant close to me, holding out the thermometer stiffly. She seemed to fill the night sky. "You're sweating," she said.

'"You're hurt," I said.

'She stared at me, and frowned.

'"The horse threw you off?" I said, speaking with the thermometer in my mouth.

'She stepped back a pace and her eyes grew wide. "My heavens!"

'I gazed at her confused brow.

'"How did you know that?" she asked.

'But already I was falling back into Switzerland, trying to find the Bergli Hut in the snowy dark—'

His tale broke off.

We had just reached the top of Hay Bluff.

We paused to catch our breath.

He stood looking out over the vast scene below, his nose hawked to the breeze, his old plaid hat fluttering at the edges, his new blue nylon jacket pressed by breeze to his thin frame. His eyes were squinting and there was a faint smile on his thin lips, and he gave a snort of laughter as if he did not quite approve of what he was about to tell me next.

'And then came the hard part,' he said.

'The hard part?'

'Waking up,' said Holmes.

'So how did you get there – to St Bart's?'

'I was found by two British hikers at ten thousand feet, frozen in the glacier. One immediately recognized me and cried, 'That looks like Sherlock Holmes!' When the ever-efficient Swiss arrived on the scene an hour later, they too saw the resemblance and contacted the Home Office in London. Very quickly Scotland Yard and Dr Ronald Coleman of St Bart's were brought into the case. I must tell you, Wilson, that Dr Coleman is one of those scientific researchers who, like Victor Frankenstein, leaves one unsure whether he should be praised or put in gaol. For years he has been obsessed with creating life, human life, and he has created a huge edifice of theory as to how this could be done by highly technical methods. No stitching together of old body parts, collected from charnel house, for Dr Coleman. He believes a human being can be designed from the ground up on a computer, every cell and strand of DNA, every part of his body calculated and then created from raw chemicals. People are already calling him mad or immoral for contemplating such a thing. Coleman admits that his theory is a few decades away from being a practical scheme. But of course he leapt at the chance of resuscitating a dead Englishman. Which was me. Apparently the dehydration I suffered as a result of becoming sick from drinking Zimmerman's concoction, plus the sudden freezing caused by tons of snow encasing me, caused my body to be freeze-dried more or less like the raspberries or peas one buys in modern grocery stores.'

The idea sounded so fantastic that I could not help but believe it, while pretending not to. 'Come now, Holmes!' I laughed.

'That's how Coleman explained it,' he said, in a tone so uncharacteristic of the man that I felt a little sorry for him. A puzzled and bewildered tone.

'Well,' I said, 'I've heard of a boy who fell into the Red River in North Dakota in the winter of 1987, and was underwater for forty-five minutes, and later revived. They said the frigid water had slowed down his bodily processes, and that is what saved him. So I guess it makes a little sense.'

'The sudden freezing was the key,' said Holmes. 'Coleman directed the whole operation. They cut out the block of ice in which I was encased, used snow-cats to haul it up to Eismeer Station, then loaded it into a converted train car, and so brought me down the mountain to where a refrigerated lorry was waiting to bring me to London. At St Bart's I was put into a specially built refrigerator where I was kept until Dr Coleman had prepared his chemical bath.'

'We'd better start back down,' I said, 'It gets dark early these days.'

'Right,' said Holmes.

We descended the steep path from the top of the bluff to the parking lot below. The world seemed huge and bright. Over the valley a tiny paraglider swooped like a drunken fly. We crossed the parking lot, stepped over the edge into green pastures, descended easily through the world of sheep as Holmes resumed his explanation.

'Stem cells derived from my bone marrow were inserted into my inner organs. There they transformed themselves into the appropriate sort of cells for each particular organ, and grew to replace the damaged tissue. The technique

Coleman used was, in essence, similar to that used by researchers in the United States who have managed to grow, for instance, a totally new rat's heart where none existed before. In my case, the scaffolding of all my organs was there, and the trick was to time everything properly, so that the total blood transfusion, the first beating of my heart, the awakening of my brain, and so on, all came together at the right moment. The whole system, or most of it, had to *come on line*, as they say nowadays, at the same time. And most of it did. There was a pancreas problem for a while, but that has been sorted out.'

'I have done many news stories on cloning,' I said. 'But I take it you weren't exactly cloned.'

'Not at all,' said Holmes. 'A cloned human might have physical characteristics nearly identical to those of the original, yet the clone would be different because he would have different memories. In my case, Coleman merely used a technique to create new cells for the existing creature. I am the old Holmes, with the old memories. My memories were preserved in chemical form in my brain while I was frozen, and those memories were revived when I was awakened. As I understand it, all human memory is preserved in chemical form.'

We walked together down and down. Holmes swung his walking stick in lively fashion. The gimpy leg did not seem to bother him except when he had to heft it stiffly over the stiles. At one point we sat down on a steep slope and looked down as dusk began to creep over the valley. He sighed. His mood changed. He said, 'I don't know, Watson . . .'

'Wilson.'

'I don't know if the game has been worth the candle.'

'No, I suppose not,' I said. 'But it's an experience.'

'Yes, yes,' he agreed. 'And yet . . .' he trailed off.

'And yet, you have lost your life,' I said. 'Is that it? Your real life.'

'Yes. I think you may have put your finger on it.'

'But you'd have lost your life anyway,' I said. 'We all do.'

'But I'd not have remembered it,' he said.

'Ah, there's a point,' I said. 'You'd not have felt lonely.'

'My fear is less of loneliness than of boredom. If a man lives long enough, he is bound to get bored. Don't you think so, Watson? An experience that is magical the first time around is routine the tenth, and tedious the twentieth.'

'Yes,' I said. 'I fear that is so. I remember, for instance, my first trip to Paris was wonderful. The fourth was still fun. Later, Paris was fine, but expected. A bit ordinary. And the lovely first bloom is now forever vanished.'

'Men have always,' said Holmes, 'dreamt of living forever – thoughtless men. I suspect, Watson, that even if the body of a man stayed as perfect as that of a twenty-year-old, stayed healthy forever, his mind would petrify from sheer boredom after two hundred years. And he would want to kill himself. To die.'

I wasn't entirely sure I agreed with him, so I was a little evasive. 'Like so much we think we want,' I said, 'I suppose eternal life might turn out to be a dreary prospect. I feel better when I avoid thinking too deeply on these sublime topics.'

'Poor Zimmerman,' he mused. 'Poor Professor Zimmerman. He died not knowing that he had experienced all the youth that a man could ever experience. He died denying the gift of mortality.'

'Movement, motion, saves us as we grow old,' I said.

'Exactly right! We must be up and doing.' He sprang to his feet and brushed himself off. 'We must be up and doing with a will to work and wait.'

'Away, then,' said I, and again we started down the hill.

'Good old Watson!' he cried, and he swung his stick at a thistle.

'You might just as well call me *Watson* and let it go at that,' I said. 'It will be easier than me having to correct you all the time.'

'Fair enough,' said he. 'Anyway, as Juliet observed, *What's in a name?*'

'Quoting Shakespeare now?' I cried. 'You surprise me, Holmes!'

'I'm afraid that my dear Watson – may he rest in peace

– left out a great deal about my personality,' said Holmes. He laughed loud, and his laugh echoed out of the trees.

We descended to the village. We walked rather stiffly to our Cambrai Cottage. We cooked a small meal, and ate it. We went weary and happy to bed.

NINE
Lestrade Presents a Problem

The Mystery of the Black Priest, as we had come to call the case of the blood bath at The Old Vicarage, weighed heavily on Holmes. 'My first case in ninety years, and I can't crack it,' he said one morning, and he laughed bitterly. I could see he was becoming desperate and depressed. Several times I had noticed him eyeing the small morocco case containing his hypodermic needle.

'Never fear,' I said. 'A tiny piece of information will come your way, and suddenly the whole case will crystallize, and you will solve it as brilliantly as ever you did.'

'I wonder,' he mused. 'I wonder.'

'By the way,' I said. 'I met Sergeant Bundle when I was buying the newspaper this morning. He mentioned that Jenkins has returned to his cottage from Scotland.'

'Ah!' cried Holmes, springing to his feet. 'Perhaps we should go see him. There may yet be hope of fresh facts.'

We drove to The Old Vicarage in my car. Jenkins was still in his silk pyjamas and dressing gown when we knocked on his door. He graciously invited us in. He was a dapper man in his forties. He had bright green eyes, blond hair worn with studied dishevelment, and he threw his right arm into the air whenever he became excited about one of his own observations.

'I was in Scotland and I have three friends who were with me to prove it,' said he. 'I am astonished, Mr Coombes, that you bring the subject up. I have gone over it all with Sergeant Bundle. I can tell you this, if I had a young boy visit me, I might well invite him to bathe with me. But I certainly wouldn't try to drown him in anything but love.'

'Do you know any actors who speak Pashto?' asked Holmes.

'I know several actors of Afghan descent, though I'm not quite sure whether they can speak the language. They are perfectly English, so far as I am aware. I doubt that they have ever been to their homeland.'

'Would they know about this house of yours in Wales?'

'They might. I throw parties here for people in the London theatre world, and word gets around . . .' He shrugged.

'Would you mind writing out the names of the Afghan actors you know?'

'It would be my pleasure, Mr Coombes.' He produced a paper and pen and, with a flourish, he wrote out a list of names.

'Thank you,' said Holmes.

'You know,' said David Jenkins, turning so suddenly that his silk robe swished. 'You remind me of someone, Mr Coombes.'

'Really?' said Holmes, in a tone that suggested he was pleased.

'But I can't think who. Wait, I have it! William Gillette,' he cried, whirling and pointing his arm at Holmes affectionately, while smiling a 500-watt smile: 'The actor, William Gillette!'

Jenkins rushed to a cabinet. He drew out a curve-stemmed meerschaum pipe and thrust it into Holmes's hand. He touched Holmes delicately, a finger on each shoulder, and turned him like a mannequin. He viewed him in profile. 'Perfect!' he cried. 'You are, without the shadow of a doubt, William Gillette!'

Holmes looked at me, seeming puzzled.

'Gillette,' I said, 'was an American actor and playwright who gained fame and fortune in the early part of the last century by writing and starring in plays about Sherlock Holmes.'

'Have you ever acted, Mr Coombes?' asked Jenkins. 'Perhaps it is time for a Holmes revival.' He moved closer to Holmes and looked at his face intently. 'Of course, you're a little long in the tooth. But make-up does wonders.'

'I begin to think,' said Holmes, 'that Sherlock Holmes has been revived one time too often.'

'Nonsense!' cried Jenkins, as he poured himself another cup of coffee. With a silent gesture of eyes and hands, he offered us each a cup. But we refused.

'If you revive a man enough times,' said Holmes, 'he is bound to disappoint.'

'Oh, Mr Coombes – what a view of life you take! A Holmes revival is always a success!'

Jenkins struck poses and launched witticisms as he ushered us to the front door and bade us adieu.

Holmes later checked out the names on Jenkins's list. They led to nothing. Two of them weren't even Afghans, but Indians.

I spent the next day reading a book that Holmes had recommended, *Martyrdom of Man* by Winwood Reade. Holmes, meanwhile, flung himself first into one chair, then another. I could see he was fading fast, and that soon he would be again in the depths of boredom and despair. This was an aspect of his personality that Watson, writing a century ago, had often mentioned. Holmes, I concluded, suffered a version of manic depression – or, as I believe they now style it, *bipolar disorder*. But beyond this was something new. He now seemed to have self-doubt. I had always thought of him as one who believed entirely in his own abilities, one who knew absolutely that if he were provided with even the slightest chance for success he would succeed. I wasn't at all sure that this was still true. It might have been true most of the time, but not all the time. Not in certain dark moments.

He lurched out of a chair and stood at the window. 'Maybe the facts are before me and I don't see the obvious.

Maybe I need more facts. A single fact, when properly viewed by the intelligent mind, ought to reveal its antecedent, which should reveal the fact before that, and back, and back, till we see the beginnings of the universe! Yes, yes, but that is extreme. Inductive reasoning can only lead so . . .' He flung himself, with an air of exhaustion and exasperation, into the easy chair by the hearth. 'You know, Watson, I have almost concluded that I'd rather be lucky than good.'

'I should hope so!' I said. 'Many a man who has worked hard, acted bravely and thought logically has – for lack of a little luck – failed utterly.'

'What I fear, Watson, is that this may be just such a case. You know, I must tell you something: not all my cases were solved.'

'Naturally not.'

'In the annals of crime, many a criminal has done his dastardly deed and skipped away to live a happy life.'

'Of course,' I said.

'Even among the murder cases I have undertaken, some were never solved and the murderers never paid for their crimes. There was the affair at Notting Hill in 1890, in which the man and his dog were both dissolved in acid. The only facts ever discovered about the murderer were that she loved the poems of Wordsworth and that she could not correctly pronounce the words *fissiparous* or *autochthonous*.'

'Really?'

'Yes. And then there was the bizarre *Case of the Shrinking Dachshund*. That was what Watson intended to call it. He even wrote it up. But his wife convinced him it was too horrible a tale to present to an unsuspecting public, particularly as it was a tale not only without a point or a moral, but without a real beginning or real ending. There was also the case, back in '97, of the Christmas tree candle conspiracy, in which the candles were tampered with and the angel on the top of the tree exploded, resulting in a whole family being burnt to death as they opened their gifts

– a case so outré and grisly that the newspapers of the time would not even print it. I could not solve it, Watson. I couldn't! I lacked one fact. Of course, the bothering thing about an unsolved case is that one can never be absolutely sure whether the failure is due to lack of facts or lack of insight. I tell you, Watson, you are right! So much is chance, so much is . . .'

At that moment his mobile phone began to play *Für Elise*.

He held the phone to his ear. He frowned. Slowly he closed the phone and put it into his pocket.

'What's wrong?' I asked.

'That was Scotland Yard. My contact there wants to see me.'

'A problem?'

'Could be . . .' He trailed off. He looked worried.

'Look, Holmes,' I said. 'Tomorrow is your doctor's appointment in London anyway. So you'll kill two birds with one journey. No use worrying about things. A change is as good as a rest. Do you good. Get away to London for a day or two.'

'Yes, yes, that's right,' he murmured. 'Quite right . . . say, uh . . .'

'What?'

'I wonder, Watson – would you like to accompany me to London?'

'It would be a pleasure,' I said.

His proposal really did suit me perfectly. A few days in London would make a nice change from rural life. Accordingly, we drove early the next morning to Hereford, caught the train, and by eleven were at Paddington Station where a black car was waiting to take us to the offices of New Scotland Yard. At Scotland Yard I finally laid eyes on Holmes's so-called 'contact.' He was a lean man about our age or a little older, with thinning black hair untouched by grey. He moved quickly out of his chair to greet us – 'Good morning, Holmes – and you, sir, must be Dr . . .'

'Mr . . . Mr James Wilson – how do you do.'

'I am Detective Chief Inspector Lestrade.'

'Lestrade!' I cried, despite myself.

'Or a reasonable facsimile thereof,' remarked Holmes, with uncharacteristic puckishness.

I tried to back off a little, to excuse my outburst. I said very mildly, 'Are you two playing a little joke on me?'

'No, no,' said Lestrade with a brisk smile. 'But I can see why you might think so. Evidently you are familiar with Mr Sherlock Holmes's personal history, as so eloquently recorded by his good friend, Dr Watson.'

'I am,' I said. 'And I am aware that in the very first chapter of that history, titled *A Study in Scarlet*, a certain Mr Lestrade of Scotland Yard appears.'

'He was my grandfather,' said Lestrade. 'He was just twenty-eight years old when he met Mr Holmes in 1880. Grandfather married late, and might not have married at all had it not been that Holmes saved a young shop girl named Mary Bates from the clutches of white slave traders who intended to ship her to Burma. Mary Bates was my grandmother. My grandfather's first son, my father, was born in 1910 when Grandfather was fifty-eight. My father went on to serve many years as a London policeman. I was born in 1942 when my father was thirty-two. And now, at the ripe old age of sixty-six, I may soon retire – I've lingered on far longer than most of my contemporaries, I fear. But I like the work, you see? That's three generations of Lestrades with careers at Scotland Yard.'

'Congratulations!' I said. 'And do you have a son to carry on the tradition?'

'My daughter Agnes works in this same building, different floor.'

'Congratulations again,' I said.

'When Mr Holmes was revived,' said Lestrade, 'the doctors learnt of his connection to my grandfather, and thus to me. They asked me to be his liaison with Scotland Yard, and to be his counsellor and guide as he oriented himself in a world rather different from the one he was

– shall we say – frozen out of.' Lestrade winked at me, proud of his wit. 'It is I who arranged for Mr Holmes to begin his new life in Hay-on-Wye under the watchful gaze of an old acquaintance of mine, Thomas Bundle, who promised not only to keep tabs on Mr Holmes, but to use him on small cases as they came along, part of our programme to help him to get back˙ in the groove while also learning a bit about modern police methods. We agreed it would be best if Mr Holmes started out in a place that was not quite the madhouse London is these days. You may imagine, Mr Wilson, what an honour, not to say a joy, it has been to me to meet the man about whom I had heard so much all my life, and who – if truth be told – was largely responsible for my grandfather's successful career.'

Holmes modestly batted away this compliment with the back of his hand, brushing his fingers through the air. 'If I helped Lestrade clarify a few small points in several of his cases, it was my pleasure entirely.'

'The reason I wished to see you today,' said Lestrade, 'is to ask if you would be good enough to help *me*, Mr Holmes. For the past week I have been troubled by a few small points in a very odd, not to say bizarre, case. In truth, I can make neither head nor tail of this strange affair at Croxley Green – yet I am certain that something dreadful is about to occur in the household of one Colonel Davis. That is why I have asked you here. I would like your opinion as to whether Colonel Davis is in danger.'

Until this moment Holmes had been languidly attentive, a bit *dégagé*. Now suddenly he sat up in his chair and his eyes became bright. 'Yes, indeed. Pray, Lestrade, give me the details.'

'The case may be of particular interest to you, Holmes, for it contains elements similar to the case you have been consulted on in Hay-on-Wye.'

'And what are those points of similarity?' asked Holmes.

'First, the Croxley Green case – Colonel Davis lives

near Croxley Green – centres on an American serviceman. Second, it involves a recently published book called *Abu Ghraib: Torture and Betrayal*. Third, it involves the supposed appearance of a black, hooded figure.'

'Go on,' said Holmes anxiously. 'Spare no detail.'

'Colonel Anthony Davis of the US Army was posted to London a little over a year ago, from Iraq, as interim military advisor to the US Embassy's Defense Attaché Office. He rented a large manor house in the countryside near Croxley Green. It is a fine house in a peaceful neighbourhood, yet his wife has never been happy there. The reason? She believes the house is haunted. Evidently the poor woman has always been drawn to the supernatural fringe – goes in for séances, regressive psychic readings, that sort of thing. She also frequently attends spiritualist meetings, for she likes to talk to the dead.'

'Then she ought to enjoy talking to me,' said Holmes.

'Come now, Holmes!' laughed Lestrade.

'A morbid wit has he!' said I.

'Anyway, a neighbour who lives near the Davises informed Mrs Davis that the house is haunted by a murdered monk, and ever since that moment she has been on the verge of a nervous breakdown. The story goes that in the basement of Tetchwick Manor a monk was tortured and murdered more than 300 years ago, in or about 1678. That was an age when cries of 'No Popery' were in the air, and when some people saw a papist with a bomb behind every tree. In those days papists were often persecuted, officially or unofficially. Mrs Davis claims that early one morning, shortly after she learnt of the ghost, she heard the ghost prowling about in her basement. This happened just after her husband had left for work. Mrs Davis was still dozing in bed and heard footsteps on the stairs. At first she thought it must be her husband returning for some reason. She called his name. He did not answer. She heard the footsteps continue upward. The footsteps came down the hallway, approached her bedroom door. She was so paralyzed with fear that she closed her eyes. According to Mrs Davis, the ghost entered her bedroom.

She dared not open her eyes. The spectre approached her bed. When she felt it actually slip into her bed with her, she began to pray to God, and that did the trick. A moment later she felt the ghost's presence vanish. Several mornings afterward the identical thing happened again: the ghost crawled into bed with her, she prayed, and it vanished. Then the ghostly appearances took on a new character. On many afternoons a black, hooded figure peered into her dining room window, always at about three o'clock. Her husband, Colonel Davis, became so alarmed at her reports, and at her behaviour, that he stayed home from work one afternoon just to prove to her that her fears were groundless. Unfortunately, he was in the loo when the ghost appeared. He heard his wife shriek, and he ran to her as quickly as circumstances would allow. She was nearly hysterical by the time he reached her. She informed Davis that only a few moments ago the tortured monk had appeared at the window. The creature had – she shrieked this – fled away, floated over the hedge, and flown off almost with the speed of a bird down the public footpath that passes in back of their house. "He flew into the trees!" she cried. Colonel Davis instantly ran in hot pursuit. He ran down the back garden path, through the gate, and out on to the public footpath. He says he could not have been more than thirty or forty seconds behind the ghost. He ran towards the grove of trees through which the path passes before it emerges again into fields. About fifty yards into the grove of trees he met a neighbour. He asked the neighbour if he had seen anyone running along the path. The man replied that he had seen no one.'

'But could the ghost have run off the path and into the trees?' asked Holmes.

'That is possible,' said Lestrade, 'but not terribly likely, for the path is fenced with a high wire fence on both sides at that point. The fence is a few yards into the trees, so it could be that the man was hiding in the trees, not far from the footpath.'

'And what do you know of the neighbour?' asked Holmes.

'Nothing,' said Lestrade. 'It was the same neighbour that had informed Mrs Davis of the tradition that her house was haunted. So one would suppose that if a ghost had appeared he would have been among the first to recognize it.'

'Touché,' said Holmes. 'But did he himself believe in the ghost?'

'I gather he did,' said Lestrade. 'Mrs Davis says it was he who told her the monk had actually appeared to people.'

'What else about the neighbour?' asked Holmes.

'He apparently is a friendly sort, lives about a quarter mile from the Davises. He encountered the Davises at a church function a month or two after they moved in. He even brought them a housewarming gift, tried to help them adapt to English life. He showed Mrs Davis the best places to shop, that sort of thing. She often met him on the public footpath when she took her morning walk. He also met her at several spiritualist meetings, and she seems very taken with his kindness. She had always heard that the English are aloof, but this man, Simon Bart, proved to her we have our welcoming side.'

'What was the housewarming gift?' asked Holmes.

'The housewarming gift?' asked Lestrade, a little taken aback. 'That is a detail which, I regret to say, I failed to inquire about. Do you think it could be important – to this case, I mean?'

'Details,' said Holmes, 'are like piles of old nuts and bolts in a drawer. You never know which one is important until you need it.'

'Excellent, Mr Holmes. Excellent. I begin to see why criminals of the Edwardian era found you such a formidable opponent.'

'I frequently stressed to your grandfather,' said Holmes, 'the singular value of cataloguing all details – a point with which your grandfather agreed in theory but sometimes neglected in practice.'

'Ah, well, Grandfather did his best, I'm sure,' said Lestrade, patiently.

'When I first met him,' said Holmes, 'I confess I thought your grandfather very lightweight, very misguided and somewhat irritating. But later, my dear Lestrade, I grew to enjoy him greatly. In later years on many an evening he stopped by Baker Street and filled me in on the latest activity at Scotland Yard, and smoked his cigar, and presented me with little problems to amuse me. I guess I mellowed.'

'We all do, we all do,' said Lestrade.

As I watched these two talking, however, it seemed to me that if Holmes was 'mellow,' I didn't know the meaning of the word. I had seldom known a man more tightly wound, or a creature with nerves so close to the skin.

'Pray, go on,' said Holmes, and he placed his index finger vertically across his pressed lips, and leant forward a fraction, listening intently.

'Three days after the colonel chased the ghost,' said Lestrade, 'Mrs Davis became so frightened and dis-traught that they decided she should take the advice of her neighbour and go for a month to a spiritualist retreat in California. Two days later Colonel Davis took her to Heathrow, dropped her off, and then went to work. When he returned to Tetchwick Manor that evening he was surprised to find, on the dining room table, a book about the horrors of Abu Ghraib prison in Iraq. The book was called *Abu Ghraib: Torture and Betrayal* – in fact, the same book you encountered at The Old Vicarage cottage in Wales. The sight of the book on the table made him uneasy. Suddenly he had the feeling that someone else was in the house with him – so much so that he called out, "Hello! Anybody there!" At that instant the doorbell rang. Colonel Davis walked towards the front door. But he never made it. Someone jumped him from behind and smashed him on the head with one of the silver candle-stick holders on the dining room table. Davis turned slightly before he got hit, and he had the impression that he might have glimpsed a figure draped in black behind him. But now he doesn't know for sure. He is now of the opinion that this "black figure" vision was just his imagination playing tricks on him.

'Colonel Davis awoke in a pool of his own blood. On the front porch he found a basket of food and a note indicating that this was a care basket from friends. They had stopped by because they knew Davis would be a bachelor for a while, and they wanted to start him off with a good meal. I have interviewed the friends, a couple who also work at the embassy. They said they saw nothing unusual at Tetchwick Manor. They noticed the colonel's car in the driveway but assumed, after they had rung several times, that he must be out for an evening walk through the fields. They had an engagement elsewhere, so they put the basket of food on the porch and left.'

'Was anything stolen?' asked Holmes.

'A few things only. Two Persian miniatures were taken from the dining room wall and a few netsuke carvings were taken from a nearby display shelf. Davis had acquired the netsuke while stationed in Japan and he was very upset that they had been taken. Also, the book was gone.'

'What were his duties in Iraq?'

'I did not inquire into his exact duties,' said Lestrade.

'It is possible they might be of some relevance,' said Holmes.

'We will need to find that out,' said Lestrade.

'Where is Colonel Davis now?' asked Holmes.

'St George's Hospital, by the Wellington Arch.'

'Keep him there,' said Holmes.

'You think he is in danger?'

Holmes's face looked grave. 'A great deal of danger, Lestrade. I should like to talk to him, if he is able, and then visit his house.'

'Apparently he'll be in the hospital for another day or so,' said Lestrade. 'You are welcome to talk to him. He is a strange man. I cannot say I like him. He likes to control people. My duty is to protect him, but he makes this as difficult as he possibly can. He will not accept any suggestions

I offer to him. I think you may expect the same reception. Good luck.'

'By the way,' I said, glancing at my watch. 'Time is fleeting, Holmes. You have an appointment with your doctor at St Bart's in an hour.'

TEN

Holmes Remembers the Horses

At St Bart's Hospital they took lab samples from Sherlock Holmes, measured all his vital signs, gave him a stress test. He passed his exam with flying colours. As we walked through the halls of St Bart's it was obvious that a number of people were in on the secret of Coombes's true identity. Doctors and nurses smiled, winked, looked at him furtively. Holmes had told me that the reason he had wanted his identity kept secret was that he did not want to become a celebrity, or a sideshow, before he was fully prepared. He wanted to adapt himself, and to make himself fully ready to cope with this new world. He felt it was inevitable that he must someday admit to the world that he was Sherlock Holmes, but before that day arrived he wanted to prepare himself fully. The people who had brought him back to life were honouring his wish for secrecy – for the time being. Yet, clearly, many of them knew. One young nurse came up to him and said, 'Sir, could you sign your name in my book?' And she presented him a first edition of *The Hound of the Baskervilles*. 'My great grandfather was Sir Henry Baskerville,' she said.

Holmes asked, 'Shall I sign it *Coombes* or *Holmes*?'

'Oh, sir,' said the young woman, and she smiled shyly.

'I recognize you,' he said. 'You were with me when I first opened my eyes.'

'Yes,' she said.

'Yet I never saw you again.'

She winked at him, and smiled a gorgeous smile. 'Other duties.' And hurried away.

Holmes insisted that I sit in on his interview with Dr Coleman. Coleman was the man who not only had engineered his resuscitation but was solely in charge of his recovery and progress. Coleman was already well-known in the medical field, and no doubt was preparing scientific papers that would make him even better known – papers describing his latest triumph, resuscitating a man who had been frozen for roughly ninety years in a glacier. For all I could guess, this was enough to win him a Nobel Prize. Then again, who knew? Every day in the newspaper one read of new research victories in cloning, tissue engineering, tissue regeneration, regrowing organs using stem cells created from an individual's own skin cells, and so on. Reviving a detective frozen in a glacier had its sensational aspects, certainly. But I suspected the public would not be terribly surprised that such a thing *could* be done, only that it had been. As to whether people nowadays would remember Sherlock Holmes, I doubted it. I suspected his fears of suffering from celebrity were unfounded.

Dr Coleman was a large and very cultured man with a shining manner and silvery hair and a basso profundo voice. He was modest and yet assertive in his exquisite politeness. He was a big physical specimen. He looked to be the sort of man who would get things done by the persuasive method if possible, by the brute force method if necessary, but get them done he would – precisely the sort of tactful and resourceful man required to arrange for an Englishman encased in ice to be brought from Switzerland despite all legal and physical obstacles, and then to arrange to have him resuscitated despite all ethical, medical and technical problems.

After Holmes had introduced me, we all took a seat in the consulting room. Coleman was beaming with affability and with pride as he gazed at his latest accomplishment. 'You look good, Mr Holmes, and all your tests look good, as well.'

'I don't feel too bad for a man a hundred and fifty-four years old,' he replied.

'Come now, Holmes, come now!' boomed the doctor.

'And you look good yourself, doctor,' said Holmes. 'I see your wife has yet again extended her stay in Italy.'

'Yes, yes, that's true. And you, Holmes, have surprised me yet again with your powers of perception and deduction . . . and I suppose –' he laughed graciously – 'I suppose I should now ask you *how* you know that. Well, then, I'm asking.'

'I know because your nurse, Miss Devon, is living with you.'

'Really, Holmes, do be polite, if you can!' He waved his arm brusquely. 'Let us get on with our business here, and enough of . . . but wait, I must say, I *am* curious. Whatever makes you think such a thing?'

'You both smell of horses,' said Holmes.

The doctor laughed – a little nervously, I thought. 'Well, that proves, at least, that the olfactory lobe of your prosencephalon has been brought back to full function, and then some,' he said.

Holmes turned to me. 'The good doctor has shown me his lovely house in Hertfordshire, and his stable of horses, and the paths where he rides early each morning before coming to work.'

'Yes, yes,' said Dr Coleman, looking now a bit uncomfortable.

'And then,' said Holmes, 'there is the matter of the few strands of cat hair clinging to the inner dust jacket of Miss Devon's book, the book I just signed for her – it looked very like the hair of your Angora.'

'Is that *so*,' said Coleman, looking now distinctly irritated.

'And of course, you both have identical tans, far different than the pale November skin of most of your colleagues, so I presume you have been a week with Miss Devon in the West Indies, where you have told me you prefer to seek your sun. You flew there?'

'Yes, yes, Holmes. We flew.'

'I should like to try flying in a heavier than air machine sometime,' said Holmes. 'I've only flown in a balloon.'

'What!' I interjected. 'That's something I never knew about you. I don't think I ever heard of that.'

'Possibly not, possibly not,' said Holmes mildly. 'Watson

did not write up everything about me. Not by a long chalk.'

'I think I may have created a monster,' laughed Coleman, leaning back grandly in his chair, and brandishing his pad elegantly.

'Like Frankenstein's monster?' mused Holmes. 'Well, there is truth in that. I sometimes feel, as he did, rather lost in a world not mine.'

Dr Coleman glossed over this psychological observation, which seemed almost a cry of loneliness. He discussed all Holmes's tests, then asked him a series of questions. Together the two of them concluded that all seemed perfectly satisfactory except that Holmes's left leg still gave him a good deal of trouble.

As we stood up to leave, Dr Coleman said, 'We have noticed before, Holmes, that your sense of smell has been greatly sensitized by your awakening – and I don't know why. But I wish to assure you that usually I take a shower after riding and before coming to work. But this morning something came up, and we had not time. I do apologize.'

Holmes had been headed towards the door. He turned back to face Coleman. 'My dear doctor, I find the scent of horses not in the least offensive. On the contrary, I rather like it. It brings me back to a time past – I have only just this moment realized it! The smell of horses, yes, wonderful! It is one of the things I miss most from those days before the Great War. You know, doctor, the world used to be full of horses. They were everywhere, and everyone in the country or city knew horses, smelled horses, had a hundred encounters a day with horses. They pulled our ploughs and our hay wagons in the country, they pulled our coaches and carriages and hansoms in the city – and our omnibuses and freight wagons. The horse was a part of our world, a part of our lives. But how suddenly he vanished! A world without horses seems to me very strange. And a little cold. Yes, I think that is the word. Cold.'

By the time we left St Bart's it was rather late to visit

Colonel Davis, so we took a taxi to our hotel in the Strand. As we ascended to our room overlooking the Thames I said to Holmes, 'You seem to have developed a poetic impulse that was unknown to you previously – all that rhapsody about horses and times past.'

'Yes,' agreed Holmes, 'I surprised myself. It just came upon me. Sometimes smells do that. They throw you back into memory as nothing else can do.'

'That's true,' I said.

He looked out our window at the Thames.

'Do you realize,' I said, 'that this is the very room where one of your famous contemporaries stayed, Claude Monet?'

'I didn't know he'd stayed at the Savoy,' said Holmes.

'He painted the Waterloo Bridge and the Hungerford Bridge from here,' I said.

'Ah,' said Holmes, still gazing at the river and the two bridges. 'I didn't know that.'

That evening Holmes spent a good deal of time surfing the Internet with my laptop computer. I was surprised he knew how.

In the morning we took a taxi to the hospital and visited Colonel Davis in his room. Davis was sitting up in a chair but he did not look particularly well. He stood shakily to greet us, then sat back down quickly. He said he was dizzy from his concussion. He was a tall man, quiet and bland. Supercilious. And cold. And dull. I wondered how he could have risen to the rank of colonel. Then again, maybe that's how. I reminded myself, anyway, that he'd just been bashed on the head. No doubt that took something out of him. There was something about his manner, though, and his look, that made me instinctively dislike him. I wasn't sure what it was.

'Lestrade said you'd be on this case,' said Davis. 'He said you have wide experience.'

'Roughly a century wide,' said Holmes.

'I'll take your word for it. Any progress?'

'I need just a little information, and then I may well make some progress,' said Holmes.

'Fire away,' said the colonel, staring straight ahead.

'What were your duties in Iraq?'

'I had a number of duties over a four-year period.'

'Let us start with your last assignment.'

The colonel hesitated. 'Why, is that important?'

'Details always are important, colonel. If you don't intend to be candid with me, I cannot help you. You were in a position of some authority at Abu Ghraib prison, is that not so?'

The colonel froze a little, and gazed at him bitterly. He was not used to being talked to bluntly. Finally, he said, 'I was in charge of a number of departments at the prison, yes. How do you know this?'

'If one searches the Web in the right way, facts emerge. Did you ever come into contact with prisoners?'

'Not usually.'

'I didn't ask that,' said Holmes. 'I asked, did you *ever*.'

'Occasionally, yes. I suppose you are asking this because of the book that appeared in my house.'

'Yes,' said Holmes. 'That is why I'm asking. Surely that was a curious coincidence, was it not?'

'I thought so,' said the colonel.

'What possibilities occurred to you?' asked Holmes.

'That someone might have put it there to irritate me.'

'Any suspects?'

'It occurred to me that my wife might have put it there – but I don't see how she could have. She went out the door ahead of me that morning, and I am almost certain that there was nothing on that table when I left.'

'Did your wife object to what you did at Abu Ghraib?'

'Yes.'

'Strongly object?' asked Holmes.

'She went almost berserk on the subject.'

'And she is now off to . . . ?'

'Someplace in California for a spiritualist psychic meditation training conference of some sort. She will be incommunicado for a month. That, she says, is part of the training.'

'And she is going to this session mainly to get away from the ghost of the murdered monk?'

'I am afraid that is the case,' said Davis. 'She needed to get away, that was for sure.'

'How old is your wife?'

'Thirty-eight.'

'How old are you?'

'I really don't see the point of this.'

'You are wasting my time, colonel. Details matter. If this is a secret and you don't want to answer, just say so.'

'I am fifty-six.'

'It was your neighbour who first informed her that the house was haunted?'

'Yes, Simon Bart.'

'What is your impression of him?'

'Very upper-class English, judging by his clothes and accent. Perfect gentleman. He has attended séances with Rebecca – that's my wife. He's into this spiritualism thing to some degree. Very thoughtful. He was the one who suggested she go away for a while after this last haunting business. Very thoughtful fellow. He came by with a house-warming gift after he realized we were new in the country. Couple of expensive silver candlesticks. Wish he hadn't. Whoever did this to me –' he pointed to his head – 'cracked me with one of them.'

'Do you know what he does for a living?'

'I haven't talked to him much and I don't know. He may be independently wealthy. He doesn't work regularly.'

'How old?'

'Forty, forty-five. Looks young. Thinks young. You know, I hate to break this up, but I'm getting a little dizzy, Holmes.'

'Colonel, it is my belief that you are in grave danger. I suggest you do not go home even if the hospital releases you.'

'They won't release me for another two or three days. But then I will go home, Mr Holmes. I'm an Army man. US Army. I am not used to cringing and cowering. I think a burglar got me, and that's that. You can bet he won't get me again.'

'I wouldn't count on that, colonel. But do as you wish. Meanwhile, would you give me permission to enter your house and look about?'

'You may certainly do that. The house key is there, on the dresser behind you. Just send it back to the hospital tomorrow.'

Holmes took the key.

'One last question: did your wife have these hysterical tendencies, these unstable tendencies, before you moved to London.'

'Yes. I am sorry to say she has been unstable all her life. But she has gotten worse since we moved to England.'

That was the end of the interview. As we left the hospital I asked Holmes what he made of the situation. He answered that it would be imprudent to make anything of it just yet. More facts were required. Then he seemed to drift into outer space. He wasn't hearing what I asked. 'How do you feel about the colonel?' I asked.

'Do you mind if we stop by our old lodgings in Baker Street for a moment?' he asked.

'*Your* old lodgings,' I corrected him. 'I do not mind at all.'

'After a glimpse at the old place we'll be off to Croxley Green.'

'I am at your disposal, Holmes!'

We hailed a cab by Hyde Park and soon were spinning up Park Lane towards Baker Street. When we arrived in Baker Street, however, Holmes was discontent. He said the area looked nothing like he'd remembered it. When we found 221B, he was astonished and disconsolate. He said it was not really the right place, though the number was plainly on the door. We went inside and found it was a museum – a Sherlock Holmes museum. Evidently Sherlock Holmes fans came here year after year to gawk.

'How odd that they remember me still,' he said.

'You were a bigger celebrity than you thought,' I answered. 'Bigger than *I* thought, frankly.'

Holmes stepped to the desk, rather awkwardly, and said to the girl, 'Hello – I'm Sherlock Holmes.'

She laughed. 'Of course you are,' she said. 'You even look like Sherlock Holmes. Here, would you care for a Sherlock Holmes map of London?'

ELEVEN
Tetchwick Manor

Holmes was in almost preternaturally high spirits as we descended into the Underground at Baker Street. We boarded the northbound Metropolitan Line train. Beyond the huge carriage window advertising posters stared at us brightly. Then they began to slide, to blip, to blur – they vanished in a slap of blackness. We passengers sat all bathed in light like objects on display in a shop window, swaying like tulips, and Holmes's eyes darted boldly over the people in the carriage, one by one, stripping them of secrets they didn't even know they had . . . or so I imagined.

'We rode this line often,' said Holmes, turning his head slightly to look at me slantwise.

'We?'

'Watson and I.'

'I didn't realize the Underground existed back then.'

'Oh, yes. In fact, it was pretty much the same as it is now, although it was steam-powered. The Metropolitan Railway began in the 1860s I think. They electrified it in '05. At the time we wondered whether electricity would be strong enough to pull a train. Lighting a bulb and pulling a train did not seem the same thing.'

We slid to a halt in the Northwick Park station.

'Next is Harrow-On-The-Hill,' said Holmes.

'For a man who hasn't ridden this line in ninety-five years,' I said, 'your memory is astounding.'

'Fear does that. Last time I got off at Harrow-On-The-Hill we were trying to crack the Archibald smuggling ring. Lestrade was with me, and Watson too. We were looking for a big dog with a diamond-studded collar. We carried revolvers, all three of us. And we needed them. I was completely in the dark about what was really happening until the last moment when Elsie Frilling's wig slid and she turned out to be Tom Turk, the most dangerous killer in London.'

'So what happened?'

'I had to use this—' He tapped the right pocket of his brown overcoat.

'Holmes!' I cried, and then I hushed my voice to a whisper. 'I hope you haven't got a revolver in that pocket – they are now illegal in this country.'

'So Lestrade told me,' replied Holmes, coolly. 'But the law missed me. It can't be applied retroactively. When I vanished in 1914, Watson and Lestrade went down to my little place in Sussex and collected my belongings – among them the Webley in my pocket at this moment, my reserve revolver. They thought I must be a prisoner of war and would return eventually, so they took my clothes, books, violin, notebooks full of newspaper clippings, syringe in its morocco case, revolver, cartridges and so on, and Lestrade stored all these things at Scotland Yard in a labelled container. His grandson, the man you just met yesterday, produced all these stored items for me when he met me on my release from Dr Coleman's care, but since I had no place of my own just then, I left most of my belongings in his care for the time being. I did want my revolver, however. I pointed out to young Lestrade that I had owned the revolver before the law was passed, and that the law therefore did not apply to me. I am not sure of the legal merit of my argument, but he allowed it. He slid me the revolver and said – and I think I quote exactly – "Get it out of sight, Holmes, and don't shoot yourself in the foot with it."'

'My heavens, Holmes. Do you really think you may need that revolver today? Do you intend to bring someone down with it?'

'A dirty game is afoot, Watson. Colonel Davis's days may be numbered if we fail to intercept the man who is playing it.'

'And what sort of person are we looking for?'

'The facts are still circling in my mind like geese, Watson, and haven't found a pond to land on.'

'You've gotten quirky with your metaphors in your old age.'

'How very astute of you! I've noticed the same thing. Many of my ideas seem queer to me nowadays. I'm not sure all the chemicals of my brain remained precisely in their proper configuration.'

We rode in silence past Harrow-On-The-Hill, Pinner, Moor Park. All the stops blurred together in my mind like the posters that blurred as we sped away from each station. I looked at Holmes and could not tell whether he looked innocent, worldly or both. According to Watson's account, in the old days he was rather a cold fish, though with a number of endearing quirks. And this was about right. He made such grand efforts to suppress all sides of his mind and personality except the logical side that at times I could not tell whether naïveté or perversity had the better claim. Could he really imagine there was any great advantage – presuming it could be done at all – in draining away all the warm impulses of the human heart and soul, leaving only the cold machinery of calculation to crank away unimpeded by distraction? He sat very straight in the bright modern seat. The huge glass window of the shining carriage held his half-reflection. He wore a brown coat and corduroy trousers and brown leather shoes, and he wore an expression that made him look somewhere between happy and amused. His sharp profile could make me imagine a hawk about to dive on its prey, or an old uncle with a quirky sense of humour and a bag of candy in his pocket for the kids. Also, he wasn't completely on the side of logic. He did have this new theory about the necessity of illogical poetical leaps in the logical process. So it really wasn't true, I thought, that he was one thing. Just mostly one thing. And this made it all the more surprising and rewarding when suddenly, amidst all his enumerating and filing and compiling of facts, he suddenly paused and just frankly admired (for a brief moment) the loveliness of the thing he was observing, irrespective of its relevance to 'the case': a footprint in dark soil. A face in a train car. A sudden baffle of wind that wakes the mind.

We stood in the blowing street outside the station at Croxley Green. The air was fresh, the leaves half-fallen from the trees, the sun lazy and hazy. We paused at a promising pub to eat a ploughman's lunch. It was a warm place, old wood and mirrors and a ruddy-faced tapster.

'The English Pub will last forever and never changes much,' said Holmes.

At that moment his cell phone began playing *Für Elise*. He flicked it to his ear. 'Holmes here. Yes, Lestrade . . . We are at this moment about to set out afoot from Croxley Green to have a look . . . yes . . . Well, I can't say for sure just yet, but I expect to have enough facts within a few hours to be able to explain everything pretty convincingly . . . Watson and I will be staying the night at Tetchwick Manor, in all likelihood . . . yes . . . we have a key . . . No, no, by no means! The assistance of Scotland Yard would be fatal to my plan! . . . I realize, yes . . . I realize I've been saying that for a hundred years . . . I'm afraid it is true in this case. Must not scare away the lion, you know, before the trap is baited . . . of course, of course. Goodbye, Lestrade.'

We paid our bill and set off walking. In examining my Ordnance Survey map I discovered we could cut off half a mile by following the public footpath instead of the road, and this we did. We spotted the typical little PUBLIC FOOTPATH signpost. It pointed us across fields towards Saratt. Soon we were walking between hedges, up a hill, along a stream. Holmes knelt and plucked a mollusc shell from the bank. As he did so his revolver pocket bulged.

'Tell me, Holmes. How much danger is involved in this enterprise?'

'Considerable. If the information we gather in the next hour or two is what I hope, we may soon encounter the man who created that blood bath at The Old Vicarage – and his intention will be to create another here.'

'Always bright and cheerful, Holmes!'

Holmes looked at me grimly. 'It may be more risk than

you need to take, Watson. I'm used to this sort of thing, you're not. When we've had our little walk through this lovely Hertfordshire countryside, you may like to go back to London and wait at the Savoy.'

'In for a penny, in for a pound,' I said. 'I risked bullets and bombs in Afghanistan. I can certainly risk an adventure with a friend.'

The path ran cheerily through meadows still misty green, past streams mottled with floating yellow and red leaves, through leaf-fallen woods where the path was bright and the trees were beginning to look cold and forlorn.

'I shall be interested to hear your "take" on this little case, Watson.'

'I am totally mystified, Holmes. All I can say is that Colonel Davis has more problems than he thinks. Sex is in the air, Holmes. His young wife is evidently having a bit on the side with Mr Simon Bart, the ever-helpful neighbour.'

'Really?' Holmes looked at me in surprise and raised an eyebrow. He swatted a mushroom with the walking stick he had grabbed in the woods.

'She meets Simon Bart at a church affair, then at a spiritualist meeting. They spend time walking together. He brings gifts to the family – supposedly for the family, but they are candlesticks, more a gift for a woman than a man. And how do they arrange to get away together? She conveniently becomes so hysterical over a supposed ghost – a ghost that *he* told her of – that this provides her an excuse for her to go off for a 'spiritual cure.' My guess is that Simon Bart is with her. How does that sound?'

'I think, Watson, you have got it . . .'

'I am flattered, Holmes!'

'I was about to say, I think you have got it *about one-eighth right.*'

'Ah,' I muttered, trying to recover as best I could. 'I am flattered to hear you say even so much as that.'

'She may well be infatuated with Bart,' said Holmes. 'And that is the one-eighth you have right.'

We noticed a pretty cottage peeking out of the trees off

to our right. In the full foliage of summer we might not even have noticed it. Autumn smoke puffed gently out of the chimney, making little smudges on the blue sky. Holmes spotted a woman, and he waved.

She was walking with a rake in her hand. She waved her straw hat and came towards us smiling. Despite her grey hair and her obvious age she reminded me of a young girl – smile on her lips, dancing blue eyes. 'Hel-lo!' she said. 'Wonderful day!'

Her name, she said, was Violet Anthem.

Holmes engaged her in conversation on trivial topics. I was surprised at how good he was on trivial topics, when the job required it. Then he modulated into a series of seemingly random questions about the sweetness of the neighbourhood. He asked directions to Tetchwick Manor, and he asked if she knew of a man named Simon Bart. Violet Anthem informed us quite happily that Tetchwick Manor was just a few hundred yards further on, and Mr Bart's cottage, Swale Cottage, was only a quarter mile beyond that, just beyond a copse of mature trees and down in the swale. She said the Davises, an American couple, lived at Tetchwick now. She had met them and thought them charming – well, the wife was charming. The husband was a bit, you know, military. The husband didn't look happy, said Violet Anthem – who looked very happy. She did not know much about Simon Bart, except that he often walked along this path quoting poetry.

'Poetry?' said Holmes.

'Poetry, oh my, yes. He speaks it beautifully. English poetry. Keats, lots of Shakespeare. I weed in my garden, he walks, and I hear snatches of his recitation. Quite marvellous, really.'

'Then he is an actor?' asked Holmes.

'I think that is so,' she replied. 'I believe I heard someone say that he was. Judging from his voice, he certainly could be.'

'Have you known him long?'

'Oh, no. Let me see, the Davises moved in about a year ago, a year last September, and then a month or two later

Mr Bart bought Nancy Deveaux's cottage – bought it or rented it, I don't know.'

'Then he is a new resident?' asked Holmes.

'Rather new. A great many new people are moving in everywhere, isn't that so? The countryside is becoming crowded, don't you think?'

'Then I wonder how Simon Bart knew Tetchwick Manor was haunted,' said Holmes.

'Haunted?' She smiled up at him, and shielded her eyes from the sun with her small hand.

'Somebody said it was haunted.'

She laughed. 'I don't think so. I've lived here forty years and I never heard that it was haunted. Of course, every place is haunted these days. I suppose it gives a house character, to call it haunted.'

We left Violet Anthem to her gardening and continued along the track until the ivy-covered walls and thatched roof of Tetchwick Manor appeared.

'The insurance rates,' I said, 'must be astronomical for a large house like that with a thatched roof.'

Holmes strode along with an abstracted look on his face. His left leg seemed perfectly cured, as if the injection of a perplexing problem into his brain had somehow deadened the aches in his body. He gazed towards Tetchwick Manor with a faraway look in his eyes. 'Everything is coming clear, Watson!' he said. 'Perfectly clear! Before long I think I may be able to put all the pieces together. Then we can stand back and admire the picture.'

'I do hope the picture does not include a blood bath,' I said.

'Ah, Watson. We must bait the trap carefully, very carefully. For a start, if we should meet a man who might be Simon Bart on this path, we must merely say hello and pass on. Let us not call attention to ourselves.'

'Right.'

We had now reached the garden gate of Tetchwick Manor and had stopped and were looking into the grounds. Leaves had blown over the driveway. The place looked tranquil and lovely. On the small pond a duck cruised.

'When we enter the place, Watson, we must be certain
that we do not speak, and we must walk very softly. No
noise. But before we go in, let us first have a look at Mr
Simon Bart's cottage.'

We strolled along the path, up a little rise and into a
copse of trees. On either side of the path we saw the high
wire fences that Lestrade had mentioned. 'So this is where
the black-robed figure, supposedly seen by Mrs Davis, so
utterly vanished,' I said.

'Not supposedly,' said Holmes. 'I am quite certain she
actually saw a black-robed figure.'

'Yet I get the impression the woman is a bit delusory,' I
said.

'She is no doubt delusory in many circumstances,' said
Holmes. 'But not in this one.'

We emerged from the leaf-fallen woods and descended
into a little swale and soon we were passing a white
cottage with red shutters and window boxes full of fading
geraniums.

'My heavens,' said Holmes. 'What sort of a vehicle is
that? I have never seen such a thing.'

'Marvellous, isn't it?' I said. 'An E-type Jaguar, vintage
about 1965. I have always thought it the most beautiful car
on the road. And that baby blue colour is absolutely striking.'

'That is the missing piece,' said Holmes.

'What?'

'We now have everything we need, Watson, to solve the
Mystery of the Black Priest, and the blood bath at The Old
Vicarage!'

'All the facts!' I said. 'An E-type Jag tips the scales?'

'Pretty much,' he said. He could not conceal a note of
pride in his voice. 'Before the night is out we shall have
laid hands on The Old Vicarage murderer, and I hope we
will have prevented a similar murder at Tetchwick Manor.
Let us continue on around that hill ahead, and then make
our way back to Tetchwick Manor without passing Simon
Bart's residence again. I think I noticed a way, in looking
at your map, that we can cut over to the side road. Let us
pick up some food at that little shop we passed in the village,

and then I must make a telephone call to Colonel Davis. And then, my dear Watson, we shall wait several hours in Tetchwick Manor and, with luck, bring this dangerous game to a close.'

TWELVE
The Torturer of Iraq

I knew, from reading the old Watson chronicles, that it was Holmes's habit to keep his cards close to his chest. He would spread his astonishing revelations on the table only after he had safely in hand the whole sequence of startling events and deductions that would allow him to 'go out' and end the game. To shift metaphors a little, only when he had found the last little stone in the mosaic, and was ready to cement it into place, would he reveal the whole picture to his breathless companion – in this case, me. I resolved to be patient.

We walked down a blowing road carrying paper bags containing bread, cheese and wine for supper. As we turned on to the Public Footpath, Holmes put in a call to Colonel Davis. I only heard bits of the conversation for my feet were crunching in leaves and the breeze was blowing and high overhead a small airplane was moaning through the gauzy sky. I heard Holmes ask where the car key could be found, and I got the impression that the colonel was supposed to call him back at a certain time. Holmes then gave me some careful instructions.

We soon reached the rear of Tetchwick Manor. This time we opened the gate and hastened to the house. Holmes inserted the key in the front door and a moment later we were inside. Instantly Holmes put his finger to his lips, reminding me that we must walk softly and not talk at all. We crept through the house. Holmes found a car key hanging on a hook. He pushed the garage opener button. We went out through a side door. Holmes instructed me to back Colonel Davis's yellow Volkswagen Beetle convertible out of the garage into the driveway, and to park it so it could be seen both from the public footpath behind the house and the road in front. This I did. The convertible top was down, which somehow made it appear as if someone had just jumped out of the car. We closed the garage door, entered the manor, and again stole through the house as silently as a couple of intruding field mice. Directly to the dining room we went. There Sherlock Holmes, with great care, silently lifted one of the silver candlesticks on the table and set it next to the matching candlestick. Very quietly we sat down to await the colonel's call. Holmes had told me he was to call at precisely three o'clock.

The phone vibrated, Holmes pushed the button. Instead of putting the phone to his ear he held it next to the two candlesticks. Colonel Davis's voice came loud and clear over the phone: 'Hello, sir, thank you for calling. I just got home. Yes. Yes. I feel a bit tired . . . The chief inspector warned me to lock my windows, and the doctor warned me to eat sparingly and go to bed early. So I will follow doctor's orders. I plan to be in bed by ten o'clock. So if you need me, call me before ten o'clock, right? After that I'll be asleep. Right. Goodbye.'

Holmes closed the phone, looked at me, put his fingers to his lips. He motioned for me to open the door to the back of the house. I did so. He carefully lifted both candlesticks from the dining room table. He tiptoed past me and out into the garden, down the path, and to the pond. He submerged both candlesticks in the shallows at the edge of the duck pond. Then he returned to the house, seeming relieved. 'So far so good,' said he.

Holmes specified a few other household arrangements that he felt must be made. When we had finished these chores he said, 'Now, Watson, let us see if we can find a potato or two in the pantry, and add baked potatoes to our evening repast. Baked potatoes, brie, bread and Bordeaux – what could be a healthier meal?'

We retired to the great room with a bottle of wine and two glasses. 'What pleasant surroundings Colonel Davis has managed to acquire for himself,' I said, waving my hand at the room in which we sat. It was a vast room with timbered ceiling, leaded windows, and a large fireplace that was, at the moment, dead. The setting sun threw red light through the windows and the light flowed grandly over the burgundy carpet like splashed wine. A few shelves of leather-bound books lined one wall. A large impressionist painting by Pissarro hung on another. These things gave the place a lived-in look, and warmed it considerably. The coffee table made of volcanic lava, the white Greek statue of a frenzied Maenad on the side table – these and many other *objets d'art* added interest to the room, lightened its Elizabethan darkness, and made it a most pleasant place in which to sit. A fire had been laid in the massive fireplace. Holmes added a match and the room instantly bloomed with heat and became more pleasant still. With potatoes baking in the oven and each of us holding a glass of wine, Holmes concluded that the time for talk had come. He sat languorously in a wooden-armed chair, his left wrist dangling limply beyond the end of the one arm, his right hand holding the wine. He said, 'You are remarkably patient, Watson. Your restraint does you credit.'

'Yes,' I admitted. 'I have been wondering why all these strange rituals have been necessary – tiptoeing like children through an empty house, listening to phone calls to no one, flinging perfectly good candlesticks into the duck pond, not to mention drawing most of the curtains on the lower floor, turning on lights of the upper floor, and backing a convertible out of the garage so it can sit in the weather and fill up with leaves.'

'Simply put,' said Holmes, 'we are trying to make it look as if Colonel Davis has just arrived home and intends to go to bed at ten o'clock. We are, in short, inviting the intruder who intruded last week to intrude again.'

'And who might that be?'

'The same who committed the crime at The Old Vicarage.'

'I do see that many elements are similar. The *modus operandi* is the same.'

'Indeed,' said Holmes. 'It is true that the book about Abu Ghraib is newly published, and so might be expected to turn up anywhere. No great coincidence there. But when both crimes also feature men in black robes – Mrs Ogmore's

Father Pritchard, and Mrs Davis's tortured monk – the odds of coincidence decline considerably. And when both victims are American servicemen who have recently served in the Iraq-Afghanistan theatre of operations, the chances of co-incidence drop nearly to zero.'

'Would you like my amateur opinion of this affair?' I asked.

'By all means,' said Holmes, as he lifted his wine glass as if to toast me, and took a sip.

'What happened here,' I said, 'was not a burglary attempt at all. Even as an amateur sleuth I can see that. My argument would run in this fashion: Davis came home from work and surprised an intruder who, when the doorbell rang, took advantage of the situation to knock Colonel Davis on the head, grab a few small items, and escape. But why grab so little? And why did he take only items so small that they could be put into a pocket or carried under a coat – the netsuke carvings, the Persian miniature paintings? If the colonel was out cold, and the visitors had left, why would he not take a few minutes more to fill the booty bag before decamping? We have seen, Holmes, that there are multitudes of *objets d'art* in the house to attract the interest of an art thief. So I will conclude that the intruder was here for some other purpose, that he was interrupted, that he grabbed a few easily hidden items to make the whole thing appear to be a bungled burglary.'

'Excellent!' cried Holmes. 'I quite agree.'

'But you seem to suspect that Simon Bart, this man who lives down the footpath, was the intruder.'

'I am certain of it,' said Holmes.

'Come now,' I said, shaking my head. 'Bart was surely after Davis's wife. He attended spiritualist meetings with her, walked the footpath with her, gave her a gift of two silver candlesticks, and it was he who suggested that she might be so frightened of a ghost that she ought to go away to a spiritualist retreat in California. I am willing to wager that at this moment Rebecca Davis is enjoying a month in seclusion with a man her own age.'

'Possibly she is,' said Holmes. 'But that man is not Simon Bart.'

'I defer to your better instincts,' I said, smiling but feeling a little irritated at his positive manner. 'But how do you figure it, Holmes?'

'Bart has been paying special attention to Colonel Davis's wife, that is true. But the question is, why? Consider. According to the blithe Violet Anthem, the Davises moved here about a year ago. A month or two later Bart moved into his cottage. Bart began to attend the same church as the Davises. There he met them both and, as you say, homed in on the woman. He learnt she was interested in spiritualism. Lo and behold, so was he. He began to attend spiritualist meetings with her, and he managed to instil in this unstable girl the idea that her house was haunted – an idea she was particularly inclined to believe, for she believes entirely in the "world beyond the wall" where spirits dwell and are perfectly able to *talk back*.'

I laughed. 'Holmes, you have a certain innocence about you.'

'When you add to this the fact that Violet Anthem, who has lived here forty years, has never heard anything about the house being haunted, it becomes clear that Simon Bart was not trying to warn Mrs Davis, but to scare her. And why? To get her out of the house.'

'It seems to me far-fetched that Simon Bart could accomplish all this,' I said.

'It was certainly a long-shot wager, and one he had little hope of winning without being able to monitor conversations in Tetchwick Manor. He needed to know how well his scare tactic was working, in order to guess when he should make his tactful suggestion that Rebecca should get away for a while. And that is where the electronic surveillance device came in. I suspected it as soon as I heard about the candlesticks.'

'Holmes!' I cried. 'I thought electronic surveillance might be one realm beyond your expertise.'

'I have been reading, Watson, I have been reading assiduously. I have been reading with no thought to expense. My wheelbarrow cost me fifty pounds.'

'Touché,' said I.

'The moment Colonel Davis told us about the gift of two silver candlesticks I thought it an odd gift to be given by someone who was so casual an acquaintance – and who, as we now learn, had moved into his house *after* the Davises had moved into theirs. One would have thought *they* would have been the ones giving housewarming gifts. In light of all the other things I knew, I immediately suspected a bug. And I was right, Watson. When I carried those candlesticks out to the pond I saw the bug as clear as day when I tilted one of the holders upside down and let sunlight shine into the hollow base.'

'So all our tiptoeing was done before you were even sure there was a need!' I cried.

'If the deception was to be done at all, it had to be done immediately,' said Holmes. 'It was a small matter to have Colonel Davis call me and pretend to be talking to someone else. Anyone listening on the other end of a bug would seem to hear the colonel's voice here in the house speaking to someone at the other end of the phone line . . . or phone wave, or whatever one would call it. The colonel played his part sufficiently well. My guess is that Simon Bart has a sound-activated recorder that starts up whenever noise in this house reaches a certain level. So he will hear Davis's little soliloquy, will know he's home, will know Davis plans to go to bed tonight at ten.'

'Except we will be here instead of Colonel Davis.'

'Exactly.'

'But don't you think, Holmes, that this is a matter for the police?'

'No, no! They have engaged me as a consultant.'

'But times have changed, Holmes! Times have changed!'

'In some ways, no doubt. But this is the way I do things, Watson, and I have always found it to work tolerably well.'

I could see he would not alter his opinion. I looked at my watch. 'Well, we have a couple of hours to kill. What do you think he intends to do to Colonel Davis?'

'Much the same he did to Private Calvin Hawes.'

'And why?'

'Certain elements of these crimes suggest a motive, of course. But in truth, I don't know why. In some ways it must be confessed that Simon Bart doesn't seem the type who would involve himself in something like this.'

'From what we know of him, he surely doesn't seem the type,' I agreed. 'I have always felt that.'

'What a curious cast of characters is the human race, Watson! When one thinks of a torturer the first image that leaps to mind is not of an actor strolling along a public footpath quoting Keats and Shakespeare. Oh, by the way, he *is* an actor. While on your computer last night at the Savoy I checked. He has played a number of small roles, mostly Shakespearean parts, over the past several years. He appears to be slowly making his way towards a small career on the London stage. He is one of those actors who is not widely known to the public but is doing good work.'

Holmes walked to the window. Dusk was settling in the trees. He drew all the curtains in the room.

'But the Pashto writing seems a problem,' I said. 'Simon Bart does not sound like the name of an Afghan.'

'It doesn't quite seem to fit. But we shall see,' said Holmes. 'Actors take pseudonyms.'

'The effort he has put forth stupefies me,' I said. 'I find it almost unbelievable to think that someone would spend months luring a man here from the United States in order to torture and murder him in a secluded cottage in Wales. And in the case of Colonel Davis, how strange! Bart has gone so far as to move to the neighbourhood in order to carry out his plan. What could possibly motivate this? It is beyond belief, Holmes!'

'Hate always is beyond belief. Beyond measuring.'

'Hate?'

'I fancy we are witnessing, my dear Watson, a version of that tremendous hate that we see being fuelled all over the world today by the way men treat each other. As to the specifics, who knows? Perhaps we shall find out.'

'Do you think he is working alone? Or could there be a terrorist organization involved?'

'So much depends on how one defines "terrorist

organization,'" mused Holmes. 'I suspect Simon Bart believes
that a terrorist organization is indeed involved, and that he
is the one working against it.'

With this cryptic remark Holmes fell silent for a few
moments and gazed at the flickering flames on the hearth.
Then he waved his hand in a peremptory manner and said,
'Enough speculation. We will see what we shall see. It is
dark out.'

'And what is our plan, Holmes? What role would you
have me play, if our visitor comes to call?'

Holmes's plan was relatively simple. He explained it to
me as we ate our meal at the dining room table. We waited
until ten o'clock, then turned off the lights in the house and
retired to our places. Holmes went upstairs to the master
bedroom. There he lay on the four-poster bed fully dressed.
He lay with his Webley in his right hand and a white coverlet
drawn over him. Meanwhile, down in the library, I lay on
the long leather couch in the farthest corner of the room,
far away from the French windows that opened on to the
back garden. Thus we waited. Holmes had predicted that
Bart would wait until one or two in the morning, the dead
of night, before making his appearance.

The moon came up. Its light fell through the white curtains
that covered the French windows, casting pale light into
the library where I lay. From my shadowy corner I could
gaze out on to a lawn that looked like another world, hallucinatory, immaterial, dreamlike. The black and barren trees
looked like props in a play, and the world beyond my
window seemed like a giant stage set in the shivering
moonlight.

I must have dozed, for I awakened suddenly to the
sound of tapping. I opened my eyes and saw a robed and
hooded black figure standing outside the French windows,
tugging at the handle, obviously straining to get in. Behind
the black figure were the cut-out trees, and behind the
trees was the full moon hanging white over the hill. I
leant and gripped the poker that I had placed nearby on
the rug. I watched as the black figure leant and picked
up a black case and floated away from the windows and

out on to the lawn towards the yellow Volkswagen. The Volkswagen seemed almost black in moon shadow. I arose from my couch and crept to the door of the library. I peeked out into the great hall. The embers of the fireplace barely glowed, emitting a faint fog of light. I heard the front door open. Evidently the intruder had a key. I had no time to ponder why, if he had a key, he had bothered to try the French windows in the library. I had no time to speculate about anything, for already he was floating across the room, passing in front of the fireplace. At that time of night, under those circumstances, it is easy to be frightened. Even a rational man may begin to believe in supernatural phantoms that he would laugh to scorn in the light of day. I heard a footstep and rustle of cloth, but I confess that even this did not completely convince me that I was watching a material being. The phantom was nearing the staircase at the far end of the room. I was determined to follow Holmes's instructions and to avoid doing anything to interfere with the intruder before whatever drama Holmes had planned for him could play out. I waited until the black shape had begun to mount the staircase at the far end of the room. Then I crept in slow pursuit, poker in hand.

I had just reached the foot of the stairs when I heard an explosion above. I bolted up the staircase and plunged into Holmes's moonlit bedroom.

Holmes was sitting up on the edge of the four-poster bed with his revolver in hand, pointing it at the hooded figure who stood at an angle to me. 'That was only a warning,' said Holmes calmly. 'The next shot goes directly into your skull, sir.' And then he flicked the light on.

The Mad Monk held a long knife in his left hand.

Holmes waggled the end of his revolver. 'Drop the knife – that's it. Now, Watson, if you would be good enough to retrieve the knife, yes, thank you. And next, my dear Watson, kindly remove the gentleman's black pillow slip, and I will be most happy to introduce you to Mr Simon Bart, tenant of Swale Cottage . . .'

Holmes pronounced this introduction in grand style, with

the air of a showman . . . whereupon I quickly jerked off the black hood –

'Ye gods!' cried Holmes.

I gasped and stepped back a pace.

Revealed before us was not the head of a man, but the head of a beautiful woman. Her lush red hair tumbled to her shoulders. She shook her head defiantly, nervously. Her skin was creamy and freckled.

'Mrs Davis! You have come to murder your own husband?' cried Holmes. He stared in disbelief.

'Not to murder him but to warn him!' she said passionately. 'Though I despise him.'

In her anger she was truly beautiful. (I blush to use this commonplace observation, but it was true.) Her high-boned cheeks were flushed, her lips full and red, her almond-shaped eyes almost a lambent blue-green in their depths, afire with passionate alertness. I had no doubt that her body equalled her face for striking beauty, for its shape was revealed even beneath the black robe. She was of medium height, and her skin was very fresh for a thirty-eight-year old.

Holmes recovered himself quickly. 'I must tell you, madam, that when a woman dressed in a black robe and hood creeps into her husband's bedroom in the dead of night carrying a knife in her hand, it is hard to believe she intends him any good.'

'Who are you?' she demanded. 'What have you done with my husband?'

Her voice was musical, throaty with warmth, and might have been engaging if she hadn't been shouting.

'I'm Sherlock Holmes,' he replied. 'And this is my associate, Watson.'

She ran the back of her freckled right hand across her forehead. She looked at him almost with horror. 'My God, is there no sane soul alive on this earth anymore? What mad world is this! Who are you?'

Holmes stood up and with the revolver barrel gestured towards a chair. 'Have a seat, madam. And explain yourself.'

She stripped off the black robe in a single motion and let it flutter to the floor. She was dressed in white slacks and a green blouse. As I suspected, she was gorgeous. She sat down in a graceful gesture of collapse. She sat upright and stark. 'Are you with the police?'

'In a manner of speaking,' replied Holmes.

'And why are you here?'

'We have laid a trap for someone who might intend harm to your husband – and that someone appears to be you.'

'That is not true!' she cried. 'Where is he? Where is my husband?'

'Someone broke into the house the day you left. Your husband was hit on the head. Nothing serious, but he has been in hospital a couple of days. Soon he will get out. We had a feeling that someone might mean him harm, and so we have waited here, just in case.'

'I know nothing of it,' she said, a little abashed, a little angry, a little insulted.

'Now perhaps you had better tell us why you are here.'

She hesitated a long while. At last she said, 'OK. Look. For the last three months I've been cheating on my husband. With a man who lives near here. I needn't tell you his name.'

'Simon Bart,' said Holmes.

'Oh, my god!' said Rebecca Davis.

'Go on,' said Holmes.

'I've had enough,' she said. 'That's all. I've had enough. My husband is a monster, as I've sadly discovered. And I'm done with him. He's a colonel in the army, Mr . . . Mr Holmes, is it? Anyway, I'm sure you know this, since you are here, that he is in the army. Throughout the ten years we've been married he has kept things pretty much secret from me, but although I did not know precisely what he was doing all the time, I thought he was protecting our country – I'm an American, as I'm sure you know. When I learned he has been in charge of torturing people I was shocked. He denied it at first. My god. I've questioned him, and it was all a bunch of BS he gave me, how it was necessary, how the Geneva Conventions weren't really being broken. But they were! He has supervised the torture of people day after day for at least three years. What kind of man is that? So then we moved here and all that terrible past was finished, supposedly. But it wasn't finished. I couldn't get it out of my head. He is a cold man, always was. Cold and dull. A bureaucrat. My god, I can't believe I married him. And then he showed his cruelty to me when I began fearing this house was haunted. People told me it was haunted and I believed it was haunted and he only laughed and looked at me with boredom and contempt and told me I was a child to believe such things. I told him I saw some creature in a black robe and hood peering in my windows, and he just blew it off, said I was blowing smoke. One day he became so impatient with me that he reached down to me and twisted my ear – can you imagine! As if I were a child in school. Twisted it hard and said that I should wake up. He said I must be mentally unbalanced. His face was contorted as he said this, and for a moment I thought he might hit me. He ought to have seen how frightened I was. But no. He gets angry, turns away. I was bothering him, that's all. My god, what kind of man is he? Only once did he make the faintest effort to help me – he stayed home one afternoon to see the ghost for himself, but really just to prove that there was no such thing and to shut me up because I disturbed him. He chased it down the path, but said he saw nothing. The great US Army, typically inept.

'Simon came into my life – and he led me down the garden path, literally. Simon was Tony's opposite. Kind, thoughtful, insightful. An artist, really. He would interject the appropriate line of poetry into conversations without sounding stuffy. We went to spiritualist meetings together, walked the footpaths together. We became lovers. I wanted it, he didn't at first. But then he came to like it, came to like being with me. He would talk to me. He would listen. He agreed when I told him my horror of what my husband had been doing in Iraq. I bought him a book that came out recently. I went down to London to buy it at Hatchards so I could get one of the first copies, and I read it in a single breath, and I was so horrified that I couldn't eat for two days. I gave my copy to Simon and then he went away for a few days on business and lost it, and I was so obsessed and repulsed that I bought another copy. When I departed a few days ago for my spiritualist retreat in California, I left the book on the dining room table, under a newspaper, so my husband would discover it and be horrified. And then I left . . . well, wait a minute, let me go back a bit.

'It was Simon who suggested I should get away to calm my nerves. He suggested a month-long retreat at a place he had heard of in California. My husband agreed. But at the last minute I convinced Simon to let me stay with him for a month. I said that a month with him would be the best therapy. He finally agreed. And when my husband took me to Heathrow and dropped me off to get my plane, I went instead to an airport hotel and stayed a day. Then Simon picked me up and ever since I have been hiding with him just a quarter mile from here. And it was delicious – until I found the horrible truth. This evening Simon went out to refill his prescription of beta blockers and I found this costume, the black robe and hood of the Mad Tortured Monk, in Simon's closet. I recognized it instantly. So he had been haunting me to drive me to his arms. This evening I realized what a fool I am. You can't imagine the sickening feeling when you realize that everyone . . . everyone is . . . oh, god, when you see that . . . pardon me . . . something in my throat . . . that everyone is using you, it is such a sickening feeling. Everyone who should comfort you is using you and cruel. I did not confront Simon. I only wanted to get away. That's all I want now. Simon was in one of his nervous moods tonight, asked me if I'd like to drive in moonlight in his E-type for an hour or two. I said no. So that's what he is doing now. Tooling along little roads in the light of the moon, quoting Keats and laughing, no doubt, at how he's scared me to death and made me his sex slave. I packed my bag, intending to come down here and sneak my Beetle out of the garage and drive to Heathrow and go to California and drop out. But then it occurred to me that first I would show my husband what a stupid man he is, show him how much I despise him, show him – the cowardly soldier, the dull bureaucrat torturer – show him what fear was, and warn him I was leaving him forever. I wished to see him afraid, terrified. As terrified as I was when he laughed at my fear. As terrified as he has made others. As terrified as he has made so many men – many of them completely innocent, cab drivers picked up on the streets of somewhere and hauled off and tortured . . . have you read the book? No, no, I can see you haven't. So that's it. I came in here to terrify him. And then to leave him forever. I wanted to go to the retreat I planned to go to, isolation for a month, to get my head on straight. And then to leave him forever. I've had enough. I've had completely enough.'

She stopped, breast heaving. Nervously she rubbed her hand over her lovely face.

'But you came here with a knife in your hand,' said Holmes.

'I meant to draw back the cover, twist his damned ear hard, let him open his eyes and see the Tortured Monk he had denied existed, let him see the knife. Let him scream. Before I laughed at him.'

'Madam,' said Holmes, 'there is a pad and pen on the table beside you, by the phone. Would you be good enough to write something on that pad for me?'

'What?'

'Write *The quality of mercy is not strain'd*.'

She took the pen and wrote. As she wrote she said, 'I've heard that line before. Where is it from?'

'Do you believe the sentiment it expresses?'

'I guess I do, yes. Mercy is natural, not strained.'

'*The Merchant of Venice*,' said Holmes. 'And now, madam – if you will indulge me – wad up that paper you have just written on, and throw it into that wastebasket by the windows. See if you can *hit the shot*, as they say.'

She looked at him queerly, but she did as he requested. She wadded it and threw. But missed. It bounced off the rim.

'Good,' said Holmes. 'Very good, excellent.'

She stared at him as if she thought him daft. She looked angry, confused, defeated, distraught.

'I think you should go, madam,' said Holmes. 'Go to your Volkswagen and go quickly to California.'

'Then you believe me?'

'Of course.'

'That seems strange.' She frowned uncertainly, relieved yet frightened.

'Not at all. Merely logical – go, madam, I think you had best go quickly.'

'Yes, yes I will go. I have already put my travelling case in the car. I am quite ready.' She got up from the chair and stepped over the black costume on the floor. As she reached the door she turned and said, 'Thank you.'

'Not at all, not at all,' said Holmes.

And she was gone. In another minute we heard the car start.

'Well, Holmes,' I said. 'I must say I am quite surprised you let her go.'

'Did you not think her story and her manner rang true?'

'I did. But I don't know that I'd have trusted her without a more complete investigation. After all, she came here wearing a hood and carrying a knife.'

'She was right-handed, Watson. She wrote with her right hand, she threw with her right hand. But when she entered the room and approached the bed, she held the knife in her left hand. A right-handed person would not use her left to stab somebody, but she might use it to hold a knife over a sleeping man's face as she twisted his ear with her right hand to awaken him with a dose of pain.'

'You always make your cleverness sound so simple.'

'Cleverness usually is pretty simple – just an undistorted view of the obvious.'

I looked at my watch. 'Eleven o'clock.'

THIRTEEN
Simon Bart

Holmes sprang to his feet. 'Off with the lights, Watson. There is still a chance that Simon Bart will make his move and reveal his hand. Perhaps even now he is working himself up to a grand finale as he cruises that pretty car beneath the wild November moon.'

'You definitely have acquired a poetic streak,' I said.

'When Bart sees his costume missing, and his mistress missing, he will realize that she has discerned how cruelly he has used her and that she has run off – just as she has. My guess is that he will not fear that she has returned to her husband, for he knows how much she hates the man. Am I right, do you think? You seem to be the expert on love affairs, Watson. Oh, what a mistake I've made!'

'All that is quite possible,' I said.

'How could I have made such an error!' he cried. 'And you saw it, saw it so clearly! I fear my logical powers are failing, Watson.'

'The fault is not in your logic, Holmes, but in your experience. Have you ever been married?'

'No.'

'There you have it.'

'That's it?'

'More or less.'

'I'm missing facts, really. Certain facts of life.'

'Have you ever been in love?'

'Couldn't be sure. It hurt too much.'

I laughed. 'It does that.'

'I've seen you hurting silently, Watson.'

'I should have picked a less perceptive roommate.'

'Think you'll ever get over it?'

'Doubt it.'

Holmes switched off the light. Moonlight filled the room like a mist. He lay down on his back on the bed. He looked made of stone, like a carving on a coffin lid. Motionless. The sound rose out of nowhere. 'One does what one can with the talent one has, Watson. Sometimes it is enough. Sometimes not.'

'I loved her,' I said.

I went downstairs to my watching post in the study. Slowly, as the hours passed, the moon shifted far over in the sky. Moonlight fell through new windows at new angles, changing things. I dozed, awoke, dozed. At a little after one in the morning, just as Holmes had predicted, I saw a figure outside the library window. No robe, no hood, just a dark figure of a man. The creature did not pause at the French windows but went straight past. Shortly I heard him turn the front door latch, heard the creak of the door. He had managed to copy her key, evidently. From the shadow of the library I watched him pass the now utterly dead fireplace. As before, I waited with poker in hand until he had begun to ascend the stairs, and then I cautiously crept after him. As before, a shot rang out just as I reached the bottom of the staircase – and up the stairs I bolted. Only this time the bedroom light was already flicked on by the time I arrived. Holmes, as before, sat upright on the edge of the bed with the Webley in his hand. 'So good of you to come, Mr Bart. Won't you sit down?'

In the centre of the room stood a compact figure, about five feet ten inches tall, lithe and muscular, wearing a black turtleneck, black pants, black ski mask pulled down over his head, and white running shoes. In his one hand he held a small knife, in his other a small towel. He was balanced on the balls of his feet, as if about to spring.

'Why it looks like Spiderman,' said I.

I can't think why I said such an idiotic thing under those circumstances.

'Drop the knife, please,' said Holmes.

He dropped it.

'Watson, would you do the honours?'

I picked up the fallen knife and tossed it into the corner

of the room. Then I stood in front of the man, grabbed the lower edge of his ski mask, and started to peel it upward over his head. But at that moment something startling happened. Even now I cannot quite understand the sequence. I felt myself upended. I tumbled backwards, I fell into Holmes. A black panther leapt upon us, a black arm came down hard – and Holmes gave a yelp of pain. The revolver flew away. In an instant Simon Bart had snatched it from the carpet. Revolver in hand, he leapt backwards like a cat. He pulled off the ski mask to reveal a youthful and handsome head. He held the revolver on us. He shrugged. He tilted his head in amusement. 'I was trained in karate from childhood,' he said. 'Now, if you gentlemen will be good enough to introduce yourselves, I would be very glad of it.'

I picked myself up off the bed. Holmes picked himself off the floor.

'This is my friend Watson,' said Holmes, 'and I am Sherlock Holmes.'

Simon Bart laughed. 'Yes, I am sure you are. The world is such a mad place that I could almost believe you are Sherlock Holmes. Now, don't come any closer, gentlemen, just sit down on those chairs, that's it. It is an old revolver but I am sure it is quite effective. And I can assure you that I am an excellent shot. Now, tell me Mr . . . OK, we will call you *Holmes*, if you like. How do you come to be here and to be putting us all into this rather awkward situation?'

'A few clues, followed by some elementary observations, led me to several inevitable deductions, and these pointed out the path that led directly to you.'

'Then you are the police?'

'Unofficial.'

'Unofficially then, let me inform you that I walked by my friend Colonel Davis's house this evening and saw evidence of intruders – curtains pulled in uncustomary fashion, the garage door partly open – and so I came in to protect his property. That is what has happened. His wife gave me a key for just such an eventuality.'

'With a ski mask on?' said Holmes. 'At one in the morning?

No, that won't do, Mr Bart. I believe you came to do Colonel Davis harm – rather the same sort of harm, I expect, that you inflicted on Calvin Hawes before you murdered him.'

Simon Bart froze for a long moment. He was a handsome man of perhaps forty. He looked both boyish and mature, his dark hair falling a little over his forehead. He reminded me of Omar Sharif in his younger years. His deep-set eyes were a deep brown. His face was unlined. Even under those conditions I had to admit to myself that the man had charm. A great deal of charm. He behaved with the impeccable poise of a movie character who, though in great danger, remains unflappable.

'You speak in riddles, Mr Holmes.'

Holmes sat down and waved his hand languidly. 'Oh, it is all quite transparent, Mr Bart. I am now in possession of all the main details and it will be quite easy for Lestrade and his Scotland Yard colleagues to prove them. For many months you have been corresponding via email with an ex-US Serviceman, one Calvin Hawes from Georgia, pretending to be a young girl named Lydia Languish who lives in Hay-on-Wye. You took the name from Sheridan's famous play *The Rivals* – no doubt because you are yourself an actor. You seduced Hawes into coming to a house in Hay that you knew about either because you had attended one of Mr Jenkins's parties there, or because you had heard of the place from some theatre acquaintance who had been there. You learnt that Jenkins would be away for a month in Scotland, perhaps by simply asking him, or else by talking to your friends in the theatre world. After seducing Calvin Hawes, I suspect you probably paid for his ticket to the UK, but at all events he was doubtless anxious to come here and meet the fetching Lydia. He arrived last week and you travelled to Hay to meet him. You travelled by train to Hereford and you wore stage make-up and false eyebrows and a wig to disguise yourself and make yourself look older. To while away the time you read a book just freshly published called *Abu Ghraib: Torture and Betrayal*. In Hereford you bought a bicycle at a shop in Widmarsh Street. That was your transportation in Hay. At the appointed hour you rode your bicycle to The Old Vicarage and parked it behind the house, leaning it against the back porch railing, leaving tracks in the damp earth. You then took your costume and book out of the panniers and went inside. You dressed up in your Abu Ghraib costume. While you waited for Hawes to arrive you read your Abu Ghraib book. Hawes arrived on time at The Old Vicarage, with flowers in his hand, hoping to meet a fifteen-year-old beauty who desired him. He met you instead. You met him in a black cloak and black hood. You tied his hands behind his back, put him in the bathtub and laid a door over the tub. You tortured him by running water into the tub. But then he departed from script by sitting up violently in the tub to get a breath. In so doing he put his head through one of the door's glass panes and cut his own throat. The carotid artery was severed and the bathtub filled with blood. You then used soap to write *Heigh-ho* on the mirror. Perhaps you did this to confuse investigators, or simply as a joke since in Sheridan's play that is nearly the first thing Lydia Languish says. As you were about to leave the house the phone rang. You listened as two of Jenkins's friends left a message to the effect that they were on the high hill behind the house and would be coming around in a few minutes to greet David Jenkins on his unexpected arrival home from Scotland. This made you hurry your departure. In your haste you forgot the book on the table in the entry hall. You rushed out of the house, got on the bicycle you had come on, and pedalled away down the drive and on to the road in your black robe. You hadn't gone far before you realized that pedalling in a black robe was a bit foolish, so you swerved off into the trees and took off the robe and put it back into your panniers. You may be interested to know it was just at that moment, and at that place, that you dropped your black hood. You later disposed of the bicycle – probably by just leaving it somewhere – and you returned here to West Hertfordshire.

'Your plans here were even more carefully laid, more ingenious, more elaborate, more expensive, and more time-consuming than your Welsh drama. When you learnt Colonel Davis had rented a house here, you rented Swale Cottage, close by, and counted yourself fortunate to find a place so very close to his. You learnt which church he attended and contrived to meet him and his wife by attending that same church. You then insinuated yourself into his family by little kindnesses. You gave them, for instance, a housewarming gift of two silver candlesticks, one of which was bugged. No doubt you had no definite plan at first, were content to let events unfold until you saw your chance. You went on walks with the wife. Since you needed to get her out of the house so that you could have a proper interview with Colonel Davis, it occurred to you to tell Rebecca Davis – lovely and unstable as she is – that her house was haunted. To fully convince her of this you put in theatrical appearances at her windows. On one occasion as you were running from the house, Anthony Davis gave chase. You must have been very quick-witted, for you stripped off your costume, threw it behind a bush, then strolled back in the direction from which you had just come. Davis appeared running down the path and asked you if you had seen anyone, and you said "no". This seemed to prove that Rebecca Davis was truly unbalanced. Her husband was convinced. Mrs Davis now became so hysterical that you did her and her husband the kindness of suggesting that she go away to recuperate at a spiritualist retreat. She agreed, her husband agreed, and four days ago she went.

'That same day you came to this house to deal with Colonel Davis when he returned from work. But before you could jump him, your plan was interrupted by the doorbell. His friends had arrived. So you whacked him on the head with a candlestick. When the people at the door had retreated, however, you realized that you could not have the desired interview with Colonel Davis. He was out cold on the floor in a pool of his own blood. You realized your interview must be postponed. To make the incident appear to be a bungled burglary you grabbed a few items from the house before making your escape.

'And so we come to this dark night, Mr Bart – a dark night when your bug deceived you. Men depend upon the glories of technology so often these days, and shout technology's praises with such pathetic pride, that one wonders if they have abandoned completely the art of thinking. Electronic creatures delude and dazzle their minds with pseudo-realities that are often phoney, transient and contrived. Men trust these little rulers desperately, drink from the digital streams they dump as if they were fresh springs provided by the Gods. Alas, these streams as often poison as purify judgement. The bug you used to monitor your progress in deceiving the Davises seemed to tell you that Colonel Davis had returned home from the hospital, that he was alone, that he would retire tonight at ten o'clock. And so you came. And here we are.'

Simon Bart listened to this monologue with a quiet intensity that, towards the last, faded into a kind of melancholy. By the end he seemed to be staring right through Holmes at some deeper mystery. 'And why would I have done all this, Mr Holmes? Since you are so clever, what could be the motive?'

'The answer to that,' said Holmes, 'is not only beyond my knowledge but beyond my imagination.'

Simon Bart coughed, rubbed his jaw. 'At least you are modest.'

'Only honest,' said Holmes. 'Not particularly modest.'

'It would amuse me to explain the motive, Mr Holmes.'

'It would amuse me to hear it,' was my friend's riposte.

'It will not take much time . . .' He coughed again. 'So just sit tight, gentlemen. And be good enough not to make any sudden movements.'

'You have the gun,' said Holmes. 'We are entirely at your disposal.'

FOURTEEN
An Afghan Tale

'Pardon the cough, gentleman, it ... I ... sorry. Two days ago at rehearsal I fell off the stage, if you can believe it, and I landed on my chest on a chair in the first row. Ever since I've been as hoarse as you hear, and coughing, I'll try to ... sorry.

'I won't weary you with a lot of David Copperfield detail. Yet to make sense of my little tale I must begin at the beginning ... sorry ... I can't think why I am coughing ... I was born in a small village north of Kabul. My father was Afghan, my mother American. She had been born and bred in Chicago, which is where my father met her. They moved to Afghanistan so that I could be born there – partly because my father wanted me to know my people, partly because my mother was an exuberant lass of Irish descent who was game for any adventure. In Afghanistan I grew up amidst family, crowded in little rooms. I was quite happy, blooming in the hothouse intensity and narrowness of village life. Everything seemed beautiful. Distant mountains, dust rolling in heat. I walked to school past a canal where reflections of silvery poplar trees shimmered. The schoolroom was plain, walls and a blackboard, but it seemed perfectly adequate to me at the time. I had no idea how Spartan it was. I walked home with my cousins, jumping and laughing. We were proud of things. We were proud of our family compound, for instance. Mud walls twelve feet high surrounded it. Within those magical walls were lush gardens where we ran and played and picked fruit and sought shade. The rooms of our building were intricate and numerous. At the time I thought they were huge. People, rooms, gardens, and at the middle of the confusion, my grandmother. She was the centre that held all together. She sat in the main room leaning on an embroidered cushion, knitting and telling us tales. That's how I remember her. I remember her happy. I wanted always to remember her happy.

'I was seven years old when suddenly we moved to Evanston, Illinois, a town situated just north of Chicago. My father, who had been educated in England, had taken a job as an electrical engineer for a large Chicago corporation. It was fine with me. America, the land of Coca-Cola and cowboys, sounded enticing. I had no fear. My parents had always spoken English to me, and I made the transition from Pashto to English quite easily. My school was vast, and vastly different, and full of magical things. Yet, truth to tell, I did not find it superior to my old bare-walled school. Only different. It was just a different adventure.

'When I graduated from high school I went to England to university. My father had always planned this. He had been a Cambridge man but I went to Christ Church, Oxford. While there I became an Englishman. I loved England. Love it still. I love it as Rupert Brooke loved it – shall I quote the poetry of Rupert Brooke, Mr Holmes, to prove that I love England?

'At University I was in all the theatrical activities I could manage, and when I went down from Oxford I enrolled at the Royal Academy of Dramatic Art in London. The years I spent there were the most arduous I have spent anywhere, but also a great joy. It was at this period that I changed my name from Salman Barialy to Simon Bart. It sounded like a better stage name. It sounded more British. And now I am British, for I have a British passport. I am also Irish through my American mother. I am also Afghan and American. I am a citizen of the world, as we all should be.

'For the next eight years I worked in the London theatre, making steady progress in my career. By then my family had moved to the north of England, near Leeds, where my father's company had a branch. Then came the 9/11 attacks, the war in Afghanistan, the war in Iraq. My grandfather on the Afghan side was long dead but my grandmother still lived in the old compound north of Kabul. I began to worry about her, and I resolved to go see her and, if possible, make her life easier for her. My parents thought this would be a good idea. Accordingly, I left England and arrived in Kabul. I was completely unprepared for the chaos and danger that I instantly encountered. Taliban fighters were everywhere present and nowhere visible. US troops were engaged in firefights. Bombs were likely to go off on any roadside, and bullets to fly at any moment over any street.

'When I reached my old family compound I was shocked that the outer walls were bullet-pocked. In one place the wall had been breached completely. My cousins and grand-mother were glad to see me. They put the best face on their situation, but it was obvious to me that they had already lost hope that they would ever regain their lives. I had been there a week when the worst day of my life leapt upon me. I had no idea a horror like this would ever visit me. It was a beautiful dawn, the sun rising pink over the still brown land, the liquid call of a bird falling through my window. I got up from my pallet, dressed. I went out to walk by the canal where I had walked as a boy. It was already hot. As I returned towards the compound I heard rifle fire, and I saw soldiers leaping over the breach in the compound wall. I rushed inside and found that my cousins and their families had vanished but my grandmother sat alone on a wooden chair in her usual room, leaning against her embroidered pillow. Her dog, a German police dog mix, was by her side. As I looked through the open window, three American soldiers appeared in the room. They began to question her in English. Of course, she didn't under-stand. One kicked open a side door with his boot, rifle at the ready, and looked out. They looked huge in the small room, all their equipment dangling from them, though they were not big men. My grandmother now looked terrified. She was beginning to cry but fought back the tears. She kept knitting. The dog was a big dog but she had her tail between her legs. She was trying to stand her ground but backing up till she was almost behind my grandmother. All this happened in a second or two. One of the men was pointing his rifle at the dog. Another one said, "Watch out for that dog." The third said, "Shoot the fuckin' thing if it moves."

'I rushed around and in through the door, and shouted, "Leave her alone!"

'And then the dog growled, and I could see what the one soldier was going to do, and I tried to stop him but someone put a bayonet in my chest. A gentle jab, and the blade went in and I felt a flame inside me and I went down. They shot the dog. One shot and she was dead. My grandmother, overcome with anguish and desperation, stood up – silent as death – and went for the soldier with her knitting needle, and the soldier backed away from her looking angry and confused but also frightened, and as he backed away he raised his arms that held the rifle, as if protecting himself, and as he turned away he smacked her on the side of the face with his rifle butt. She went down. I was bleeding, the front of my shirt wet with blood, but suddenly I didn't feel it and I got to my feet and grabbed the soldier who'd shot the dog – and all this while the other two were standing back a bit and watching this scene. One was laughing, but the other said "Shit," as if he weren't happy with what was happening.

'"What do you want!" I cried. "What do you want!" I sounded fairly rational. Too rational, I thought.

'I have played this scene over a thousand times in my brain. It is there forever.

'I grabbed the chin strap of his helmet, pulled him and he fell. Something fell out of his pocket. The other two men had grabbed me now. My grandmother lay on the floor.

'"Shit, he speaks English," one of them said. As if this fact had only just now registered with them.

'The soldier I had pulled off his feet pointed at the floor. "Pick it up," he said. "Pick it up you fuckin' bastard – look what you've done!"

'The two soldiers on either side of me pushed me down, forced me down to my knees. I picked up what he'd dropped. It was a pocket bible. The front loose cover fell open as I lifted it, and printed in black ugly letters on the inner cover, as if written by a retarded child, was the name *Calvin Hawes*. I never forgot that name.

'"My bible, my bible," he cried, angrily, grabbing it from me. I thought he might shoot me.

'They held me. I said, "Are you going to just let her die?"

'Suddenly rifle fire erupted nearby and they ducked for cover and ran into the next room, and I could hear them shouting and running through the compound. I went to my grandmother. Her face was bruised but nothing was broken that I could see. I helped her up. She was crying. One of my cousins appeared from somewhere, and helped her to her bedroom.

'My cousins wrapped my chest. Tied it. Then the soldiers returned and took me away. A firefight had broken out and they were afraid of being cut off from their troops. They dragged and shoved me, and somehow I fell and was on a stretcher and a medic was working on me. I was in a medical facility somewhere. The doctor said a thoracic aortic aneurysm had been caused by the knife thrust, and he looked concerned, but the other doctor said it was not a great concern so long as the bleeding was stopped. I was taken to a questioning centre of some kind, and I was called a Taliban agent. They declared that my papers were false, even my British passport. After a while they sent me to Abu Ghraib prison in Iraq. I begged for a lawyer but the Americans said I had no rights. None. I didn't know where I was, or what was happening.

'I was at the prison for two years. I was tortured daily. The more that I swore I had nothing to tell, the more they tortured me. They put me on a board and began to drown me. They kept me awake for days. In winter they stripped me and made me cold for weeks, and I slept on cement. I lost track of time. I thought I was going mad. I think I am mad now. You say you are Sherlock Holmes. Obviously you are a madman – or are you? I don't know anything anymore. The world will never be right for me again. You cannot understand how it is. It is so unbelievable that no one can understand it. For two years I wondered – in anguish – what had happened to my grandmother and cousins. At first it is the horrible injustice that keeps going through your mind. You have been raped, battered, unjustly accused,

your family smashed. The idea of injustice obsesses you.
But then the idea of injustice fades and you are just numb,
you are just trying to stay alive. And then that feeling also
fades, and you no longer want to stay alive. You want to
die. You dream of dying but you can't die. They won't let
you die.

'I heard his name first from a guard who was talking
to another guard: Colonel Davis. That was the name. It
rang around the horrid halls of the place, the barren bloody
walls. He was the man in charge. On him my hate focused.
Not on the guards who abused us, for they were too much
like animals, moles, rats in a sewer. No, my hate focused
on Colonel Davis. And one day Colonel Davis appeared.
I actually saw him. He came down to see his orders carried
out. The guards made ten or twelve of us kneel. We were
nude. There were women guards too, men and women.
Some of the men took down their pants and urinated in
our faces. Then they made us lick their . . . what! You
lurch from your chair, Mr Holmes? I'm sorry. Are you
really so delicate? It is funny. After all this happens to
you enough times, it becomes normal. Not extraordinary.
Of course, it leaves its mark. I can never in this life enjoy
sex again. Nor love. Nor hope. Nor anything. All is but
a screen of pain on to which I cast my shadow and try
to pretend I am living. I acquired social graces early in
life that linger and create the illusion that I am a more
or less normal living being. But I am dead, Mr Holmes,
quite dead. It is not even a stage on which I move, it is
a movie screen. Poke your finger through it, and there is
nothing behind.

'I will overleap the details – for your sake, Mr Holmes.
Let me only say that the guards had sex in front of us,
made us have sex with each other, rammed sticks up our
asses, and when we screamed with pain they pretended our
screams meant we desired more of this sexual pleasure.
Colonel Davis, who has in the press so adamantly asserted
that he never knew what was happening in the prison, who
has said that he was only vaguely aware, who has sworn
before a committee that he never saw anything, who has

argued that it was in fact illegal for him to participate in the interrogation sessions, who has asserted repeatedly that there really was no way he *could* have known – Colonel Davis who denies everything, was *there*. Colonel Davis, in addition to all his other charming traits, is a liar. He watched us be humiliated in every way known to man. Many times I heard guards mention that Colonel Davis had given orders. Many times I heard them say, "Don't let up on these shits, or Davis will be on your ass." And Davis, yes, Colonel Davis came down to watch the fun. Davis was very clean in his uniform. His face was shaven and sober and satisfied. I stared at his face. I memorized it. I decided to kill him.

'I was released in 2005, for reasons as random and inscrutable as the reasons I was arrested and imprisoned. In 2004 the world had learnt of how the United States treats its prisoners, so when I came out and people learnt where I had been – the few close friends I told – they believed. They asked about the black hood that was pictured in all the newspapers of the world. I said, yes, I too had been hooded. But I told them that was nothing compared to the worst they did to us. But most people I never told. It is not something one wants to tell, for to tell it makes it happen again. And again. And again. Makes it happen not only in dreams at night but in daytime whenever they ask. Then you have no respite in waking, none in sleeping, no respite at all.

'I was released, and I soon afterward learnt that my grand-mother had died less than two weeks after the Americans had abused her and killed her dog. I had expected such news, and yet it devastated me. Fortunately I had some-place to go, and though my father had died while I was in prison, he had left my family quite well off. So I had money at my disposal. The poor are simply crushed, but the fortu-nate such as I must carry on the fight against injustice.

'Do you know the plays of Webster and Tourneur, Mr Holmes, Mr Watson? *The Revenger's Tragedy, The Duchess of Malfi*. Tragedies of blood, as we like to call them, but mine would only be the last act of a tragedy concocted by

other men, that killed 600,000 Iraqis and Afghans, or more.
That sent American boys whirling into eternity, lifted into
their graves by roadside bombs, or sent them home without
limbs. Or sent them home to America (where I went to
school and loved movies and ate ice cream) half mad. I
saw once on the front page of the *New York Times* pictures
of scores of ex-soldiers who had gone home and killed their
fellow citizens. A madness has been turned loose in the
first four acts of the play, and I would write the fifth, and
madness and revenge would be my theme.

'Private Calvin Hawes of Georgia had been wounded and
sent home to recuperate in a VA hospital there. I managed
to find his email address and I began to write to him, posing
as a fifteen-year-old British girl who was, oh, so sympathetic to his plight. I wrote as a child and he responded,
and when I began to indicate my passion, and when I sent
him a photo of a delicious blonde who was supposedly me,
he could not resist my invitation. He was young, hungry,
deprived, and the madness of desire in the blood leads many
a man to destruction. I did not intend to kill him, only to
destroy him.

'It was all as you said, Mr Holmes. As you so rightly
deduced, I lured him to The Old Vicarage. Through the
window I saw him come uncertainly up the walk, with a
bouquet of flowers held behind his back. I met him at the
door in my costume and I pretended in a small voice that
it was a Halloween costume, and I spoke in a tiny whisper
and told him that I was shy, and then I told him how I had
dreamt of him, and I told him what I wanted, and I asked
him to kneel and eat me. He was trembling with desire as
he knelt – and suddenly he discovered his horrible mistake,
and he lurched backwards in an agony of revulsion, and
then I swatted him with David Jenkins's oak walking stick
which I had found leaning in a corner, and he fell to the
floor out cold. I tied his hands behind his back, and thrust
the flowers into his hands because it seemed the thing to
do, and I dragged him into the bathroom and laid him in
the huge lion-foot tub. I intended simply to leave him there,
stripped of his wallet and all his belongings, and let him

awaken to his terrors and humiliation. Then I got to thinking he should be reminded of the dog he'd shot, and the old woman he had indirectly killed. The death of the poor dog bothered me even more than my grandmother's plight. How could that be? The image seared me; a noble creature made afraid, trying to defend herself, tail between her legs, impotent, helpless, crushed, humiliated, killed.

'I waited until he awakened, then told him why he was there. He stared. I asked him questions. His answers revolted me. I grabbed a door with glass panes that I had seen leaning in the back hallway, and I laid it over the tub. I began to run water into the tub. He began to struggle. The water grew deeper. He grew tired of trying to keep above water. He gave a tremendous lurch, like a huge fish, and sat up violently, and his head smashed through the glass pane, and he slit his throat a huge gash as he fell back. The blood poured out. The tub of water turned red. I knew nothing could save him. Then the phone rang, and I heard a message that someone was coming, and I left quickly. It was all as you said, Mr Holmes.

'I had not intended to kill Private Hawes. I wouldn't have killed him. But he's dead now. And my grandmother is dead, her dog is dead, my village is dead, three of my cousins' children are dead. A lot are dead. For many, hope is dead. They live on, but they are dead.

'I had not intended to kill Private Hawes, but I did intend to kill Colonel Davis. After torturing him, of course. You see this rag I brought? With it I would have made him know he was drowning. You see this cord I brought? Oh, I have several sweet ideas for Colonel Davis, but none sweet enough to pay him for all the horror he has caused to innocent men. Have you read, gentlemen, how the army person in charge of the prison has now said publicly that probably ninety per cent of the people there were innocent? 'Tis true.

'I did intend to kill Colonel Davis tonight. I have been caught in a kind of madness. Always I have known I am ruining my own life with revenge. Revenge is sweet but only for a moment or two. Yet I cannot help myself. I'd

like to sup on horror for an hour or two more. But you
gentlemen have thwarted me . . . pardon me . . .'

Here he broke off in a fit of coughing. He had been half-
sitting on the edge of the little table in the window alcove,
with the revolver in his hand. Holmes and I sat in two chairs
across the room, facing him.

'To thwart you is our duty,' said Holmes.

'And what,' he said, 'do you think my duty may be, Mr
Holmes?' His voice was very hoarse.

'That is your affair.'

He nodded. He looked very balanced and graceful in
body, standing up straight now, his head tilting. His black
pants and turtleneck made him seem both elegant and
dangerous. 'I could kill you, Mr Holmes. Poof! Gone. With
scarcely any effort.'

'I have been dead once and it wasn't so bad. Maybe it
is even easier the second time.'

'But I can't,' said Simon Bart. He laid the revolver on
the table and walked away to the far end of the room and
turned. 'Is there no solution for my problem, Mr Holmes?'

Holmes stared at the blank window. 'I can't think what
it would be,' he said, at last.

'If you cannot see a solution, I suspect there is none.'
Simon Bart began to pace the floor. He sank into a chair
as if a weak spell had come upon him. He sat like a rag
doll, leaning far back, limp, as if someone had flung him
there. He coughed, and his voice seemed to have become
more hoarse. 'C'est la vie. "The best-laid schemes o' mice
an' men/ Gang aft agley." I had hoped to spend Christmas
with my mother.'

Holmes looked at his watch. 'You ought to be able to
make Leeds by noon, if you get moving quickly. In that
Jag of yours, maybe you'll get there even sooner.' He glanced
towards the window. 'It will be getting light soon. Watson
and I are off to Wales.'

'Holmes!' I cried. 'Think what you are doing!'

'It is all right, Watson.'

'I wonder,' I said. 'I wonder if it is all right!'

Simon Bart got slowly to his feet. He looked intently at

Holmes, as if waiting for a cue. He coughed, fell into a fit of coughing. He muffled his mouth with a handkerchief and looked at Holmes. His eyes above the handkerchief looked frightened. 'Why?'

'The first reason I shall keep to myself,' said Holmes. 'The second is that I suspect you agree by now that revenge is a poison cup, and mercy – even to the merciless – a better choice. How does it go, Mr Bart? "The quality of mercy is not strain'd, / It droppeth as the gentle rain from heaven . . ."'

Holmes stopped, seemed puzzled to continue.

Bart paced. He rubbed the back of his neck. Little beads of sweat appeared on his forehead. He was nodding, waiting, as if the unfinished quotation disturbed him – as an unresolved chord disturbs a musician. He said, '"It droppeth as the gentle rain from heaven / Upon the place beneath: it is twice bless'd; / It blesseth him that gives and him that takes . . ."' Then he trailed off, still rubbing the back of his neck, still pacing. Suddenly he halted. He looked up, as if at the first balcony, and held out his right arm – '"Though justice be thy plea, consider this, / That in the course of justice none of us / Should see salvation; we do pray for mercy, / And that same prayer doth teach us all to render / The deeds of mercy."'

Beyond the window the dawn was just breaking, making visible the twisted black limbs and barren branches of the trees, bare ruin'd choirs where late the sweet birds sang.

FIFTEEN

New Lodgings in Baker Street

A black car from Scotland Yard met us at the Baker Street tube station. Lestrade and Holmes sat in the back seat and I sat up front with the driver as we rode the short distance to Paddington mainline station where we would catch our train to Wales.

'Colonel Davis is still in some danger,' said Holmes. 'I recommend you keep him in a safe house somewhere for the month of December.'

'I will see to it,' said Lestrade. 'But he won't like it.'

'Excellent,' said Holmes.

'He doesn't like being cooped up,' said Lestrade.

'Excellent,' said Holmes.

I turned in my seat and looked at the two of them sitting side by side. I said, 'You'll have to admit, Lestrade, that Holmes is back on his old form.'

'Yes, yes, I think he is,' said Lestrade. 'Yet I sometimes wonder about his motives, a little. He is taking rather longer to lay hands on the suspect than used to be his custom.'

'This case requires more discretion than most,' said Holmes. 'I will deliver your man to you no later than January first of the New Year.'

Lestrade laughed. 'You always were a secretive sort – reluctant to reveal all that you knew till the final moment that suited you. That habit drove my grandfather almost to distraction, but always he pursued his own course, even knowing he would likely be one-upped at the end. And I am afraid, Holmes, that I, like my grandfather, must pursue my own course in this case. You say Colonel Davis may be in grave danger, and therefore we will put him on ice for a while in an obscure safe house. But my own informants tell me that the man responsible for The Old Vicarage murder is very likely a Hungarian fanatic named Franz Pistek who publishes pamphlets decrying the presence of American forces in nations all around the world. We have agents looking for him in Bratislava at this very hour, and they expect a break in the case soon.'

'That's a comfort,' said Holmes. 'With both of us working on the case, I am sure one of us will solve it.'

At Paddington Station we parted from Lestrade and not long afterwards Holmes and I were in a comfortable train carriage, sipping vile tea from paper cups and trying to pretend it was drinkable, while watching English country-side slide away behind us as we rushed towards Wales. 'Well, well, so you are not quite confident of Simon Bart after all,' I said, stirring more sugar into my tea. 'You have put Colonel Davis out of his reach.'

'Trust everyone – but always cut the deck,' said Holmes.

'And yet I'm surprised you let Bart go, Holmes. Square with me, now.'

'I let him go, my dear Watson, because Simon Bart is only a small fish, and if we allow him out of our net for a little while, it is no great loss to justice, and perhaps even a gain. For if Colonel Davis is inconvenienced by being required to live in cramped and secret quarters for a month, then I can only say that Colonel Davis has kept numerous innocent men living in cramped and secret quarters for years, while he supervised their torture – and I fear that this little inconvenience I have arranged is the only punishment he will ever suffer for his crimes. We need not be overly concerned with netting little fish like Bart, nor even blood-sucking fish like Davis. We ought to be concerned with harpooning the killer whales who have roiled the waters of the world and set up this huge pattern of death, destruction, hate and horror. But, alas, I fear harpooning them is impossible.'

'Killer whales? What killer whales? And why would it be impossible for a man of your talent to impale them and gaol them?' I said.

'You know my history, Watson, and I suppose you are remembering the clash I had with the greatest criminal mind of an earlier day, Professor Moriarty. You are remembering how, in the end, I brought him down and destroyed his whole organization.'

'Exactly so,' I said. 'Moriarty was the mad and almost omnipotent intelligence at the centre of a web of crime that entangled the whole of London. Though it took years of trying, you did finally manage to end his career by throwing him to his death in the Reichenbach Falls. His lieutenant, Sebastian Moran, the best shot in the Indian Army, then came after you in retaliation, and you collared the villain while he was trying to kill you with an air gun. If you could do it then, you can do it now. That is my point. I don't believe for a minute that your age will impede you.'

'Not my age,' said Holmes. 'The difficulty is not my age, but *the* age. We live in a different world. There are super-ficial similarities, of course, to that earlier battle against evil. In this case, too, there is a master criminal and his lieutenant at the centre of a web of crime, horror and terrorism that ravage our modern world. These two malev-olent brains are directly responsible for the death of Calvin Hawes and many another innocent victim. But I have no way, no possibility, of bringing these men to justice. They are beyond the reach of justice. They are too powerful to touch.'

His answers bothered me. I couldn't help remarking, 'Then do we simply reel in our lines and nets, stash our harpoons, and let the killers go, is that it? It isn't like you, Holmes!'

'I'm afraid we must, Watson. They will die happy, rich, and applauded by their small circle of friends. There is nothing anyone can do about it.'

'That isn't the way a story should end,' I said. 'It sends chills through my heart to hear you say it. The two evil geniuses escape! My god.'

'Not two evil geniuses,' said Holmes. 'One genius, one dolt. They lurk in Washington, DC, at the centre of a web of crime that covers the whole world. Moriarty and Moran ruined many a life in London. These two have ruined lives throughout the American Empire, which stretches all around

the world. That man Pistek, who Lestrade so foolishly im-
agines has a hand in these killings, is right. The US has
more than eight hundred military installations in at least
thirty-nine countries of the world. No ruler, no person, is
safe from the hand of the two who sit at the centre of the
web and control those forces. Those two can, if they choose,
reach out and grab almost anyone, and gaol them, torture
them, kill them. Their reach is worldwide.'

I felt my heart beating hard. 'I had not realized your
political opinions were so passionate – or, indeed, that you
had political opinions at all.'

'I have grown wiser with age,' said Holmes. 'Two life-
times does that to you.'

Holmes and I returned to our cottage in Wales and returned
to our books and study. I bought the *Pickwick Papers* first
edition that I had so long admired, and I bought many another
rare and curious volume. Holmes bought everything, filling
his wheelbarrow with a miscellany, a gallimaufry, a mélange
of the strange, the commonplace and the erudite, an omnium-
gatherum with which he educated himself about the events
of the last ninety-four years.

November turned to December. Snow fell on the barren
hills and made the world a wonderland of white. I made
black boot prints on the street as I returned down
Chancery Lane to Cambrai Cottage. Holmes had the fire
blazing. As I entered he looked up from his book and
said to me, 'Watson, all is pattern, repetition, variations
on a theme. What you have done once in life, you do
again – a prisoner of your own personality, and of life's
natural cycles.'

'Come now, Holmes – surely you exaggerate a little.'

'Not at all. I dare say, if a man lived long enough, everything in his life would repeat itself – in outline if not in
fine detail. Have you not noticed, Watson, how often you
are in a situation and you have the feeling you have been
there before? *Déjà vu*. And my belief is that in most cases
you really *have* been there before. And sometimes you can
recall the earlier situation, and sometimes not.'

'It is an interesting theory,' I said. 'But if we are really just repeating ourselves, what fun is it? What meaning could there be?'

'Why should there not be fun and meaning in repetition? You read the same book twice sometimes, do you not, Watson, and actually get more out of it the second time through? You sometimes go to the same movie twice.'

'True,' said I. 'Very true.'

'Well, there you are,' said he. 'Your life is a movie that keeps playing different but similar scenes over and over, and you enjoy it nonetheless.'

'Yes, I see your point,' I said. Suddenly his observation seemed not only clear but wise.

Yet at that very instant his own enthusiasm seemed to collapse. His face fell and the light went out of his eyes. 'Even so, one is likely to get bored,' he mused. He launched himself out of his chair and stood by the window looking out at the snow like a disconsolate child with no playmates and nothing to do. He stood with his hands in his trouser pockets, gazing out at the white little street.

He looked lost.

December leaked away and we heard nothing more of Simon Bart, and nothing from Lestrade or Scotland Yard. It was almost Christmas. I had no people to go to for the holidays, and neither did he, so we hung a wreath on Cambrai Cottage, and he gave me a book as a gift, and I gave him a book, and we unwrapped them and made a fuss – as if we didn't already have enough books! – and then we went out to Christmas dinner together. Sergeant Bundle stopped by late in the afternoon with a Christmas cake. He was ruddy with bumptious good cheer, and he thanked Holmes for his work on The Old Vicarage case. He said Holmes's work was excellent work, fine work, but some fish always get away, he said, putting his hand on Holmes's shoulder – and I could see Holmes cringe. Bundle said he doubted now that the man would ever be caught, but not to worry, not to worry. 'Merry Christmas, gentlemen!' said he, and he was gone, bustling away. And somewhere bells were ringing.

The following afternoon Holmes got a call from a private

detective in Leeds, Alfonse Smedley, who informed him that Simon Bart was dead.

'Holmes,' I said, 'you are a miracle of efficiency. I didn't realize you had hired a man to watch him. You do cover the ground pretty thoroughly, don't you!'

'One tries, one tries,' said Holmes, carelessly. 'I knew pretty well that the aneurysm would do him in. And so it did. He fell dead right on the sidewalk outside his mother's house, dropped dead as he stepped out to bring in groceries from his car. I instantly saw that his problem was still lurking, caused by the bayonet wound in the chest he had received in Afghanistan, then exacerbated by the fall from the stage. The fall must have reopened the split in the artery, and this suddenly brought on the hoarse voice and coughing that we noticed. Those are symptoms my old friend, Dr Watson, long ago told me were characteristic of some aneurysms. And of course the girl, Rebecca, mentioned that he was on beta blockers, a sign that he had probably guessed his own fate.'

'Well, you were right again, Holmes,' I said. 'Doubly right. At least the poor tortured soul got to spend Christmas with his mother.'

'A gift of Luck,' he said modestly.

'With a little help from you.'

'Hmm,' said Holmes. 'And I don't think I'll tell Lestrade the good news for a few days more – let Colonel Davis live a little longer in fear, cooped up in his safe house.'

'Holmes!' I cried, 'I'm proud of you. I had always feared you were too much a man of principle.'

'Ah,' said Holmes. 'Principle is good, but one can only stand so much of it. As Juvenal remarked, the wise person puts limits even to his honourable actions. *Imponit finem sapiens et rebus honestis.*'

'There is truth in that,' said I.

'But I'm bored, Watson. I languish. I need action. I need a dose of the world.'

'Funny you should say so,' I replied. 'I was thinking just yesterday that it might be nice to move to London in the spring.'

He leapt from his chair and grabbed an apple from the bowl on the table and tossed it in the air. 'A capital idea, Watson! Just the thing.'

'Last night,' I said, 'I was on the Web and I found some very nice lodgings in Baker Street, your old haunt. A nice area it is, close to Regent's Park—'

'Yes, Watson. Let us do it!' he cried. 'In Regent's Park we can stroll and contemplate problems! Pacing through Regent's Park with a problem on my mind was always a thing I loved. Shall we rent a place together?'

'I think we should,' said I. 'We'll be there in spring, almost like being reborn.'

'I wonder –' he mused, looking at me earnestly and full of hope – 'do you suppose Lestrade might send a few small problems my way when we're back in the city?'

'I am absolutely certain he will, Holmes,' I said, and I grabbed an apple from the bowl and tossed it, and caught it. 'How could he not!'

'Quite right!' said Holmes. 'It is perfectly logical. How could he not? After all, I have been tracking criminals for a hundred and thirty years.'

Beyond our window, snow had begun to fall. I opened the cottage door and looked out. A distant bell began to toll. As our tiny street filled up with snow I imagined I saw Mr Pickwick's coach and horses bursting round the corner in a muffled clatter. Suddenly the world, so strange and full of wonder, seemed to promise startling days of companionship ahead, and the pleasant jolt of dangerous journeys.